Jane Marion Wakefield Richardson

Six Generations of Friends in Ireland

1655 to 1890

Jane Marion Wakefield Richardson

Six Generations of Friends in Ireland
1655 to 1890

ISBN/EAN: 9783337327460

Printed in Europe, USA, Canada, Australia, Japan

Cover: Foto ©Andreas Hilbeck / pixelio.de

More available books at **www.hansebooks.com**

SIX GENERATIONS

OF FRIENDS

IN IRELAND

(1655 to 1890),

BY

J. M. R.

SECOND EDITION.

"LET IT PLEASE THEE TO BLESS THE HOUSE OF THY
SERVANT . . . FOR THOU, O LORD GOD, HAST SPOKEN IT,
AND WITH THY BLESSING LET THE HOUSE OF THY SERVANT
BE BLESSED FOR EVER."—II Sam. vii, 29.

LONDON:
EDWARD HICKS, Jun.,
14, BISHOPSGATE WITHOUT.
—
1894.

PREFACE.

—

THESE simple narratives were intended chiefly for the use of the family of whose ancestors they treat, but as the book has met with a more favourable general reception than was expected, a Second Edition is now issued, enlarged and revised.

The lives here traced are necessarily confined to a limited area in space, and were mostly passed within a small section of the Christian Church, whereas the love which inspired them was not limited by space or sectarian difference, but flowed out to meet every human need.

For several interesting particulars the reader is referred to the appendices.

J. M. R.

MOYALLON,

    7th mo., 1894.

To my Beloved Children, the SEVENTH

GENERATION of Friends in Ireland, I Dedicate

these Simple Memorials.

CONTENTS.

SIX GENERATIONS

OF FRIENDS
IN IRELAND

(1655 TO 1890).

CHAPTER I.

17TH CENTURY QUAKER PIONEERS IN IRELAND.

BEFORE entering upon the simple annals of the family whose history we are about to trace in these pages, it may be interesting to the reader to obtain some idea of the political and religious condition of Ireland two hundred and forty years ago, in connection with the introduction of Quakerism into the country.

With this subject is associated a soldier in Cromwell's army, named William Edmundson, who was born at Musgrove, in Westmoreland, in 1627. In early life he abandoned the profession of arms and entered on a commercial career. Soon after, under the preaching of a powerful minister, James Naylor,* he says:

---

* See Appendix D.

B

" My heart was opened, as was the heart of Lydia ; I received the Truth in the love of it ; I had longed after it, and was ready for the Lord's harvest."

Having obtained mercy of the Lord to be faithful, after much suffering he joined in worship with Friends, and going to live in Ireland about 1652, he was made the means of accomplishing a spiritual work, very similar to that effected by George Fox in England.

Like the founder of the Society, he united clear spiritual apprehension with strong natural character, and though of comparatively humble rank, his consistent godly life, and his impartial view of men and things, gave him a well-merited influence at the seat of Government in Dublin, during both Protestant and Catholic ascendancy. He felt through all his sufferings for conscience's sake, in as far as these sufferings were patiently borne with consistent protest against intolerance, they might become, as indeed they did, the means of a more universal liberty of conscience.

William Edmundson, on reaching Ireland,

first settled in Antrim, and then removed to Lurgan, in the Province of Ulster. It may be well to state that two centuries ago Ulster was one of the most uncivilized and wretched portions of Ireland. The plantation of Scottish colonists by James I proved the turning-point, and gradually changed the social, as well as the religious state of the country.

In 1652, the time of William Edmundson's arrival in Ireland, the country was partially recovering, under the iron rule of Cromwell, from the ruin and desolation caused by the " War of Religion," 1641, an insurrection proclaimed against the Protestants by the Roman Catholic bishops North, south, east, and west, Protestant blood flowed, and cruelties, too terrible to mention, were enacted. Towns and villages were all but destroyed; in many cases the only burial allowed was the burial of the living. In Ulster it is said 100,000 Protestants were either expelled or massacred.

When the express that brought the news was read in the House of Commons, it produced a general silence, all men being struck with horror.   When told out of doors it spread like lightning, producing terror over the Kingdom.*

Doubtless the attacking party had wrongs to redress, and political grievances, and the Protestants, in their suffering and indignation, were guilty of cruel vengeance.   It was a truly awful experience, and for eight succeeding years the wretched island groaned under the contending power of four political parties fighting among themselves in bitter animosity of civil and religious hatred.

In 1649, Cromwell, with an army of the Parliament, succeeded in reducing the country to a good degree of order.

It was among these surroundings William Edmundson found a home; here he lived and died a man of love, and a peacemaker between all sects and parties.   On his removal to Lurgan his brother joined the family, and a Meeting in their house was established in 1654—the first settled Meeting of Friends in Ireland.   Small at first, the numbers increased

---

* See Tract by George Fox: " The Arraignment of Popery," 1669.
 " An Abstract of the Massacre in Ireland."

under his care and ministry. " For," says he in his Journal, " the name of Friends and the fame of Truth did spread, and divers sober people, who sought after the knowledge of God, joined us." In 1696 the first Meeting-house was built in Lurgan; it was used by the Society until about 1889, when a commodious structure replaced the time-worn and decaying edifice where our forefathers worshipped.

In 1655 William Edmundson crossed to England to see George Fox. " I met him," he writes, " at Badgley, where there was a great gathering of Friends. After Meeting I went to George Fox. He took notice of me, and we went into the orchard, and, kneeling down, he prayed. The Lord's heavenly power and presence was there; he was tender over me. I told him where I lived, and of the openness among people in the north of that nation to hear the Truth declared, and of the want of ministering Friends in the Gospel there. Soon after this visit ministers began to come from England; Richard Clayton apparently being the first, with whom W. E. travelled

extensively on foot through a wild country.
Next came to visit Ireland two women Friends
from London, Ann Gould and Julian Wastwood. They travelled from Dublin to London-
derry, and then to Coleraine, and so through
the Scotch country to a place called Clough,
all on foot in Winter time, wading rivers and
dirty, miry ways, so that Ann Gould, being a
tender woman, was much spent. She staid
her journey at Clough, the enemy persuading
her that God had forsaken her, and that she
was there to be destroyed, but I knew nothing
of them. My brother and I being at a fair
in Antrim, as we were late, proposed to lodge
at Glenavy, six miles on our way homewards.
Before we reached Glenavy I was under great
exercise of spirit, believing my shop was in
danger to be robbed that night. I told my
brother, and we concluded to travel home,
but my spirit was still under great exercise,
the word of the Lord moving me to turn back
towards Clough. These two motions brought
me into a great straight ; to travel back and
the service unknown, my shop on the other
hand in danger to be robbed. I cried to the

Lord in much tenderness of spirit, and His word answered: 'That which draws thee back, shall preserve thy shop.' So we returned to Glenavy, and lodged there, but I slept little. My brother next morning went home, and towards evening I came to Clough, and took up my lodgings at an inn. When I came into the house I found Ann Gould there in despair, and Julian Wastwood with her; but when they heard my name (for they had heard of me before) the poor, disconsolate woman revived for joy and gladness. I saw then my service of coming there was for her sake, so I told them I was brought there by the good hand of God, led as an horse by the bridle to the place where they were; then they greatly rejoiced and praised God, and the tender woman was helped over her trouble.

"They had a mind to go by my house to Dublin, to take shipping for England, but neither could ride single, so the next day I carried them behind me, first one, and then the other, when we came to a very foul way I set them both on horseback and waded myself through dirt and mire, holding them both on with my hands. I got them to Carrickfergus, and there leaving them, I rode home and sent my brother and two horses to bring them to my own house. They staid some time and visited Friends ; my brother set them on horseback to Dublin, and so they went to England.

" On reaching home I enquired about my shop ; they told me the night I was under the exercise about its being robbed the shop window was broken down and fell with such violence on the counter that it awakened our people, and the thieves were affrighted and ran away. So I was greatly strengthened in the Lord, I saw it was His word that said : ' that which draws thee back will preserve thy shop.' "

As yet Friends were confined to Ulster, but in 1655 this work of convincement and conversion extended to other parts, mainly through the instrumentality of Elizabeth Fletcher and Elizabeth Smith, and that of Francis Howgill and Edward Borrows—they were the first to hold a meeting in Dublin. They travelled south to Bandon and Cork, E. B. preaching through the streets of Limerick as they passed along, and outside the gates addressing a great multitude.

Their ministry was so successful in gathering in persons of different classes and positions that the religious teachers became alarmed, and on returning to Cork they were apprehended, and by order of Henry Cromwell they were conveyed to Dublin by a band of soldiers, and left on shipboard under sentence of banishment.

The same day Barbara Blandon landed in Dublin, and proceeded direct to the Deputy. Those who were in waiting on Henry Cromwell tried to deceive her, introducing one of the officers to her, and uncovering the head to him. As she stood in silence, they enquired why she did not speak to their lord, she replied : " I will address your lord when I see him." On which they took her to the Deputy. She then declared the message of God, that the injury he was doing to the Lord's people would at last lie heavy on his soul, and spake with such power that Henry Cromwell seemed under deep concern, so that she perceived the enmity did not originate with him, but that the pressure which was brought to bear by Civil Magistrates and Priests stirred up this persecution.

Soon after James Lancaster and John Tiffin arrived from England and suffered severely, with William Edmundson, at the hands of the populace in Lurgan.

Also came John Burnyeat, travelling on foot. Many by his ministry were turned from their evil way and converted to God.

William Edmundson had now a call to Dublin to plead for Robert Lodge, an English Friend, and others cast into prison. "I went," said he, "to the Earl of Montrath, the Lord had given me a place in his heart, which I retained till his dying day. I received a full order to the Sheriff to set these Friends at liberty, without fee or reward; which was accomplished, though the Sheriff was very angry, and called me the devil and other bad names."

One of these travelling ministers writes: "The Lord hath in Ireland a blessed, zealous people for His Name and Truth, they are filled with love to His servants, manifested in their accompanying us from one meeting to another, from ten to twenty at a time, the distance of five-and-twenty miles, even in harvest time.

" Now at this time I travelled much, for the Lord had given me a testimony for His Truth to deliver in Meetings and public places. I met with rough usage, but Truth gained ground, and Meetings were settled for the Worship of God. I was put in prison in Armagh, but, though weak and contemptible in my own eyes, the Lord was with me; His power and dread was my strength and refuge. I continued my way through danger and hardship, being often in prison, yet many were convinced and meetings settled. In the County of Donegal I was moved to go from house to house, and still asked if there were any within who feared God. The country was mostly inhabited by Scotch people who were Presbyterians. In Cavan I was kept close prisoner in a nasty dungeon, amongst thieves and robbers, for fourteen weeks. When the Assizes came, as I was looking through the iron grate overhead, a Justice of the Peace saw me, and coming up said he was sorry to see me there. Now my enemies reported I was in prison because the Quakers were against law and Government, and were only for the Light in men. So I asked him to get me leave to come into Court before the Judge, for I had something to say, so he sent the gaoler for me, and told the people, who crowded round, to make way for the prisoner; so they made way, and I got near the Judge, but he spoke aloud, asking who I was, what I was, and why I came there ? I answered, with a loud voice, I am a prisoner for my faith towards God, and I want justice, for I know of no law I have broken, but have ventured my life to establish the Government, and I own the Government and the laws. The Judge was disturbed, and cried out to the gaoler : ' Take him away.' I was very easy in my spirit, and much comforted in the Lord, for His power was with me; and some sober professors came and said they were very glad and well satisfied with what I said of our owning the Government and the laws, for they had heard other things concerning Friends. The next day I was turned out of prison without any trial.

"We had a Meeting at Belturbet, where the

Provost carried all the men and women to prison, and next morning put me in the stocks. The people were much dissatisfied, so the Provost sent his officer to take me out, who opened the stocks and bid me take out my leg and go my way; but I told him I had been grossly abused, as though I had done some great offence, so let the Provost come himself and take me out, for he had put me in. The Provost came and bid me take out my leg. I told him No, for he had made me a spectacle to the people, and I knew no law I had broken, but let him take me out who put me in. So he opened the stocks with one hand, and took out my leg with the other.

" At this time Oliver Cromwell had put forth a declaration, that such should be protected in their religion as owned God the Creator of all things, and Christ Jesus the Saviour of men, and the Scriptures, etc. So the Governor and great men of the town would try us by this declaration, whether we and our religion were under Oliver's protection or not. The Provost was there, and I was sent for to answer the particulars. I answered them so that they gave judgment that we were under protection, and our religion was to be protected. Then I called aloud that they had been witness how long we had been illegally imprisoned, and that I had sat in the stocks in the market-place wrongfully, and that for such cases the law provided reparation. Several of the chief of them offered to be evidence against the Provost. My spirit was borne up on the wings of an eagle; that day many were convinced, several received the Truth, and abode in it.

" In 1655, it came mightily upon me to leave shop-keeping in Lurgan and to take a farm, to be an example in the testimony against paying tithes. There was one, Colonel Kempston, convinced of truth, though he did not join with Friends; he had much land in Co. Cavan, and wished Friends to settle on his land, promising to build them a Meeting-house. My brother and I rode to his house and treated with him for several parcels of land for ourselves and other Friends. So, leaving Lurgan Meeting well settled, several families moved with us to Co. Cavan, viz.,

Richard and Anthony Jackson, John Thompson, Richard Fayle, John Edmundson, and others. We held Meetings around in divers places, so that several were convinced and joined with us, particularly John Pim, Robert Wardell, William Neale, Thomas Morris, John Chandley, and many more. Thus Truth spread, Meetings settled, and many brought to the knowledge of God were added to Friends; but sufferings increased for not paying tithes, priests' maintenance, refusing to repair worship-houses, not observing their holy days (so-called); for these things they fleeced us in taking our goods, and imprisoned some of us. But in those days the world and the things of it were not near our hearts, but the love of God and His testimony lived in our hearts, and we were glad of one another's company. Though sometimes our outward fare was mean, and our lodging on straw, we did not mind high things, but were glad of one another's welfare in the Lord, and His love dwelt in us."

In the course of a few years, several in this Colony of Friends, being disappointed by the conduct of their landlord, left Co. Cavan, settled near Mountmellick in the Queen's Co., and opened a Meeting about the year 1659. The settlement they left at Cavan was broken up during the next war, Friends being driven from their homes and dispersed to other districts.

William Edmundson did not confine his life and labours solely to the country of his adoption, for we find him often in England, three times in the Islands or English Plantations in America, pursuing the warfare at his own cost—lest he should be chargeable to any man, oftentimes alone and on foot—by land and sea, in the wilderness, among wild beasts and cruel men. In 1688, he is in company with George Fox in Barbadoes, labouring on behalf of the slaves. Again, reminding Friends on the American Continent that " God made of one flesh all men who dwell on the earth, that Our Blessed Saviour shed His blood for All, and that God is no respecter of persons, having taken away the partition wall of enmity between one people and another "; so said he : " Make their condition your own, and remember a conscience void of offence is of more value than all the world, and truth must regulate all wrong."

Thus early Friends raised their voice against slavery, and continued to labour on behalf of the coloured man, until, in the year 1774. the Society cleared herself of this iniquitous traffic.

On one of these visits to America, a sudden call to return home overtook him, without any apparent cause ; informing George Fox, the latter remarked Friends were expecting him in certain quarters, and it was improbable he could find a vessel willing to put out, the sea being so infested by pirates. W. E., however, found a home-bound ship, and made a very fast passage (in three weeks). On arriving, the cause for the recall was apparent, as Friends were in much trouble through some disorder in the Church, which W. E. was soon enabled to set right.

The state of Friends in the year 1661, is thus set forth : " Now was King Charles II coming in, and these nations were in heaps of confusion. They ran upon us as if they would have destroyed us at once, breaking up

C

our Meetings, taking us up in highways and haling us to prison, so that there was a general imprisonment of Friends in this nation; I was prisoner at Maryborough with many more Friends, yet the Lord supported and bore up our spirits above sufferings and cruelties, so that Friends were fresh and lively in the Lord's covenant of Light and Life.

" Contented in the will of God, we had many heavenly-blessed Meetings in prison, and the Lord's presence was with us, to our great comfort and consolation in Him, who wrought our deliverance in His own time."

About this time, died Charles Richard Poole in Wexford Prison for non-payment of tithe, and Richard Pike in Cork Jail for conscience sake : " The memory of the just is blessed ! "

" In 1665, I, having my liberty, found a concern in my mind to solicit the Government against the priest's fierceness and cruelty, for George Clapham, priest of Mountmellick, tried to prevent the miller grinding our corn, or any to speak or trade with us or our children. He watched the market and Friends' shops, and those he saw or knew to deal with Friends he sent the Aparitor to summon them to the Bishop's Court, so forced them to give him money, they being afraid of the Bishop's Court, it bore such a great name.

" This priest told his hearers that if they met any of us in the highway they should shun us as they would shun the plague, and if they owed us anything they need not pay it, or if they knocked us on the head the law would bear them out. At which the people were mightily troubled, and in general their love declined from the priest and drew towards Friends. They would offer their servants to carry our corn to the mill, that we might get bread for our families.

" I drew up a paper, stating some of his gross proceedings, and got many of his own people to sign it. He was sharply reproved, and had been punished (for the Primate said he would make them examples) but that I said we desired nothing but to be quiet, and live at peace in our callings, so I forgave it and the matter fell.

" However, being at Meeting in Mountmellick

he sent a constable to apprehend me, and
would send me to Maryborough Gaol, but the
Earl of Mountrath superseded his warrant and
set me at liberty till the Assizes. When the
Assizes came, and the said priest stood up
against me, four lawyers, one after another,
pleaded for me, though I knew nothing of
them, or gave them any fee; but the Lord
gave us a place in the heart of the people, and
the indictment was quashed and the priest
hissed at by the Court. Many Friends who
were present greatly rejoiced in the Lord to
see these evil designs frustrated.

. " At another time this same man indicted
several of us for attending a certain Meeting,
which he called an unlawful assembly. He
also indicted me for not paying a levy towards
the repairs of his worship-house, though the
wardens and constable had before taken from
me for the same a mare worth £3 10s. Friends
thus proceeded against were fined, and an
order given to distrain our goods.

" So I rode to Dublin and petitioned the
Lord-Lieutenant and Council. I and another
Friend had a fair hearing. The Lord-

Lieutenant would know why we did not pay tithes to ministers, so I shewed him out of the Bible the law was ended that gave tithes, and the priesthood changed that received them, by the coming and suffering of Christ, who had settled a ministry on better terms, and ordered them a maintenance. He would know what maintenance they must have. I told him Christ's allowance, and I shewed him from Scripture what it was, as the Lord opened them to me by His Spirit and power, which gave me utterance, and sent home what I said to their understandings.

"There were three Bishops present, but not one replied to this discourse, though so nearly concerned in it.

"In conclusion, the Lord-Lieutenant bid God bless us, and said we should not suffer by not attending the public worship, neither for going to our own Meetings. Now this quieted the priest, and it soon got abroad that the Quakers had the liberty of their religion, which was a great ease to Friends, for we had been often imprisoned and had goods taken on this account."

After the nation had become settled, and the passions of the people began to cool, William Edmundson, having obtained his liberty for about twenty days during the general imprisonment, proceeded to Dublin, where he solicited the Lord Justices, the Earls of Orrery and Mountrath to set his Friends at liberty imprisoned in different parts of the nation, and was so successful as to obtain an order for their release; he then travelled through Ireland to see that the Sheriffs had complied with the order.

In 1669 George Fox and several other Friends came to Ireland. After one Meeting some Papists present were very angry, and raged much, whereupon G. F. sent a challenge to all the Friars, Monks, Priests and Jesuits, to come forward, and in public try their cause, but, as no answer was forthcoming, he told them they were in this respect worse than the Priests of Baal, for they were willing to try their god.

During this visit of George Fox Meetings were established for the transactions of Church affairs, which at that day chiefly had reference to taking an account of sufferings, supplying the need of those in prison, making collections for the poor, &c.

William Edmundson writes: " I was much eased by it, for these matters had lain heavy on my Spirit ; now, this gave every faithful Friend a share in the burden. I travelled with G. F. from place to place, and when he left for England I laboured in our own nation, the Lord giving me an understanding in the government of his Church."

The following passage, found in the journal of a minister named Oliver Sansom, will serve to shew the devout disposition of Friends in those days : " In 1676, the general Half-year's Meeting began on the Fourth day of the week, at the ninth hour in the morning ; the Meeting for worship continued till after the first hour. About an hour after Friends met again to consider the affairs of the Church, but the power of the Lord brake forth so mighty among Friends in many testimonies, prayers and praises, that there was no time to enter on the business of the day, and so the Meeting broke up. Next morning the Meeting began again

about the ninth hour, and continued until
about the third hour in the afternoon, and a
precious heavenly time it was, then we ad-
journed for one hour, when Friends came together again to go about the business, but then
again the Lord's power mightily appeared,
whereby many mouths were opened to declare
His goodness and to offer up prayers and
praises to the Lord, which took up the time of
the Meeting of that day also, so that very little
could be done as touching business. But early
the following morning Friends went about the
business of the Meeting, and continued at it
the greatest part of that day, when it was
concluded, viz., on the Seventh day of the
week."

The outbreak of hostilities between William
and James II led to terrible suffering, shared
by all respectable classes of settlers in Ireland,
Friends and others alike.

A party of Sir Maurice Eustace's troops
coming into the neighbourhood of Mountmellick, went to William Edmundson's house,
and, seizing him by the hair of his head,
dragged him about the yard, among their

horses' feet, without any further provocation than the fact of his not being a Papist. Some of them with clubs, and others with pistols, swore they would kill him; which being heard by his wife, she came out to them in great alarm, and desired them to take all their property and save the life of her husband.

They then left William and turned after his wife, swearing and calling bad names; shot several times at his mastiff dog, which was kept chained, and then rode off like madmen, abusing and beating all the English they met, and almost killing some.

In 1692 it was computed that the losses of Friends in Ireland amounted to £100,000; so that from England, and even from Barbadoes (where Irish Friends had preached the Gospel), money was sent to relieve poverty and suffering.

Under date 1685, when about 60 years of age, W. E. writes:

" A weighty exercise came over my spirit of great trials approaching, which would try us all, that the Lord would spread the carcases of men on the earth as dung; so, in the power of the Lord, I faithfully warned Friends and others, in many Meetings and in divers places, and often in His movings advised them to lessen their concerns in the world and be ready to receive the Lord in His judgments, which were at hand, and flee to Him that they might have a place of safety in Him. These admonitions I was moved of the Lord to publish. So I was a witness that His care is for and over His people, that they might make ready against the day of trial. And in a short time trouble came on apace.

" The Earl of Tyrconnell, then (under James II), Lord-Deputy of Ireland, armed the Irish and disarmed most of the English, so great fear came upon the Protestants, most of the leading men and many others left their places and substance and went for England, others of them got into garrisons. Soon after war broke out, and abundance of the Irish, who went in bands (but not of the army) called Raparees, plundered and spoiled the English Protestants ; also many of the regular troops were very abusive. We being sharers with other Protestants in these sufferings, a concern came upon me to appeal to the Government to redress abuses committed in the country. So I was much in Dublin, applying to the Government on behalf of the people under suffering. They would hear my complaint and gave forth several orders to magistrates and officers of the army to suppress the Raparees and refrain their abuses. I was sometimes with King James to make him aware of the calamity the Protestants were under; the Lord made way for me, and I had a concern upon me to use it for the public good, the chief of the English Protestants being gone who might have appealed to the Government for the safety of the country.

"Now was wickedness let loose and got ahead, so that through violence and cruelty our Protestant neighbours were forced from their dwellings, and several families came to my house, and every room was full. Most of their cattle that were left they brought to my land, thinking themselves and goods safer there than elsewhere. We were under great exercise and danger, not only of losing our goods but our lives.

" At the battle of the Boyne the Irish Army being beaten, many of them fled our road. They plundered my house several times ; they were so wicked and bloody my family were obliged to go out of the way.   My wife desired me to go aside, lest they should kill me, for she would have ventured her live to save mine, but I would not do it.   The Lord's secret hand restrained them, and preserved our lives, though they took our household goods and all our horses that were left.

" Violence was indeed let loose, and no government to apply to.   The English Army did not appear for some time, and we were exposed to the wills of cruel and blood-thirsty men.   So I went to the chief of the Irish near me, and advised they would use their utmost endeavour to keep off their countrymen from spoiling the English of what little they had left, and when the English Army, being masters of the field, would advance, we would then use our endeavour and interest to do the like for them.   They promised with many oaths to perform this to the utmost of their power, but did not, for there were few nights but that some were robbed or wounded, so that they who lived near us were forced often into the parish worship-house at Rosenallis for safety. When the English and Scotch arrived they began to plunder the Irish, but King William put forth a proclamation, that all who would live peaceably at home should be un-molested.

" Notwithstanding there came two captains with 300 men and drove away about 500 head of cattle and horses and prisoners, including William Dunn, a captain in the former war; his son they stript, to hang him under sus-picion of his being a Raparee. The Dunns sent for me in haste; I took horse and rode as swift as I could, having regard to my promise of neighbourhood. When the Irish saw me riding after them, they followed, hoping to get their people and cattle released.

" When the officers saw me they made a halt for they knew me. I reminded them of the King's proclamation, and said that not the soldiers but the leaders would be responsible for the injury done, that it was a reflection on the King's promise, and on the English nation. So with much discourse and arguments, the two captains seemed willing to release all, if the soldiers could be prevailed upon.

" I rode with them to the head of the party, but they were very angry, and would have killed the Irish that followed for their cattle, whereupon I dismounted and got in among the rude soldiers to save the Irish, and with much ado, I, with the captains' assistance, got them moderated, on condition they should retain a small part of the cattle and release the rest.

" Then I mounted my horse and sought out the man they had stript for hanging, I threw him my riding coat and reasoned the matter with the officers and men, telling them it was unmanly and not like a soldier to strip men in that manner, for I had been a soldier myself, and should have scorned such a base action.

" So the captains made the man who wore Dunn's clothes put them off and return them to him, so the father and two sons were released with all their cattle.

" Now the English Army settled in their

Winter quarters, and the Raparees increased their strength; they burned many brave houses and some towns, also killed several Protestants; so all was full of trouble, yet through the wonderful mercy of God, we kept up our meetings regularly. In travelling to and fro we were often in danger of our lives by the Raparees, but the Lord preserved us, so that I do not know of above four Friends in the whole nation that were killed all the time of this calamity.

" At our Half-year's Meeting in Dublin, we had heavenly-blessed, powerful Meetings, and Friends were more than ordinary glad one of another in the Lord Jesus, who preserved us alive through many dangers. In the time of the Meeting, tidings came that the Raparees had taken some 20 of my cows, but that none of the family were hurt, so I was well satisfied, for all who lived out of the garrisons were in danger of their lives.

" When the service of the Meeting was over, I returned home and found my family well; but spoil and cruelty increased, and great dangers were plain in my view, yet I durst not

remove, for I knew it would discourage
Friends and the English about us, and
perhaps cause them to flee from their habita-
tions, as many of them thought they were
safer for my staying in my place.

"So I went to Colonel Biarly, then
Governor of Mountmellick, near our home,
and told him if he did not use some speedy
means to succour our quarter, it would be to
his great damage; yet he took no notice of it.
That same night some hundreds of Raparees
beset my house, I, with my family, being
asleep. The shooting was heard at Mountmellick, and a certain lieutenant went to
Colonel Biarly, and desired a party of men to
relieve me, but he would not grant the request.
So the men set fire to my house. I staid
therein till much of it was burned, when we
could stay no longer for the fire. I made
conditions before I opened the door; these
they broke, though they had bound themselves with many oaths. What plunder the
fire spared they took, with my wife's uppermost garments, and so left her; but me and
my two sons they took away bare-legged and

bareheaded, and not much better than naked. One of them lent me, at my request, one of my old blankets to lap about me. We were led through rough places, mire, and water to the knees in cold weather. Our bare legs and feet were sore hurt, and bruised with gravel, stones, and bushes.

" The next morning they took us to a wood, and held a council upon us ; they concluded to hang my two sons and shoot me, because, they said, I was a stout man.

" I said many of them knew me and my sons, and I challenged them to prove that either I or my sons had wronged any of their country folk one farthing all these times of trouble, but on the contrary had saved them what I could, sometimes with the hazard of my own life among the English soldiers. Several said they knew I was an honest man. I told them if I died they were my witnesses that I was innocent, and God would revenge my blood. They wondered at my boldness, but my life was little to me, for I desired to die if it was the will of God. They then hoodwinked my sons to hang them. When they

D

came to hoodwink me, I said they need not, for I could look them in the face and was not afraid to die.

"Now came up Lieutenant Dunn, who knew us well; he was son of old Captain Dunn, whom I had got released, and brother to him whom they had stript, whom I got released also, as aforesaid. He had commanded the villanous party that burned my house. Several others to whom I had done kindness were also present. So this lieutenant, expecting to get preferment for what he had done, would take us to Athlone, 20 miles. Thus the Lord interposed, and would not suffer them to take our lives, having a further purpose of service for me.

" The said Dunn kept us three nights by the way at a cabin, cold and hungry, so that they themselves wondered how I could endure it, but I told them they had taken and destroyed my food, and the Lord had taken away my appetite so I was fitted for it. As we went to Athlone, Lieutenant Richard Dunn railed against us, but I told him he should not rail at us for we were prisoners, and a right soldier would not rail at a prisoner. They said they were going to burn Mountmellick. I told them there were many honest people there, and said God help them.

" As we went through Raghan there came forth of a cabin an ancient man, who looked on me with a sorrowful countenance, as though he pitied me. I asked if he would give me a bit of bread, for I knew my sons were very hungry; the man answered and said he would give me a piece of bread, if he bought it with gold, for he believed I was one that did not use to beg my bread. So he went into his cabin, and fetched as coarse a bit of bread, I thought, as ever I saw, and said he was sorry he had nothing to give to eat with it. I said it was very acceptable, and gave it to the lads. That night we got straw to sleep on, so rested well, and the next day got to Athlone*, where came the High Sheriff and a crowd of rabble and soldiers calling us traitors, rebels. and such names ; it was a wonder they did not stab us with their bayonets and skeins, the High

---

* The Headquarters of the Rebels.

D 2

Sheriff animating and encouraging them. In the interim a genteel, proper man crowded through them, and came close to me, calling me Master Edmundson, and asking how I did. I answered : ' Thou seest how I do, but I know thee not.' He spoke aloud to the Sheriff and the rest, saying : ' I have known him above 20 years to be an honest man, say you all what ye will of him.' This made them all quiet ; thus the Lord provided succour for us in time of imminent danger from their own people.

" They took us to the mainguard, where this man came and brought me refreshment, and told them they did not know me so well as he did. He acquainted me with what Lieutenant Dunn had informed against us. This man's name was Valentine Toole, a lieutenant. I heard he was reproved for being so kind to me, and durst come no more to see me.

" We were taken to the Castle, where Colonel Grace and the Council met. I came in with my old blanket lapt about me ; the Governor asked my name and where I lived.

I told him I was old William Edmundson. He stood up with tears in his eyes, and said he was sorry to see me in that condition, for he knew me well, having been at my house. The Governor spoke roughly to the lieutenant, and asked him what he brought us there for. He answered with this excuse, that the Raparees were about to hang us, and he brought us there to save our lives. The Governor said if he had them there he would hang them, so committed us to the custody of Captain Francis Dunn, and soon sent us a loaf of bread, a piece of beef, a bottle of drink, and 20s. of brass money; but we could get no straw to lie on, so lay down on the bare floor, which was very hard and cold, we wanting clothes, and my strength was much spent, therefore not likely to continue long if the Lord had not again provided succour.

" Now John Clibborn,* a Friend, hearing of me, came to Athlone, and when he saw me in that condition he cried out, wringing his hands. He went home six miles to get some meat,

---

* See p 105

but he had few clothes left for himself, having been sore plundered and spoiled.

" Now most of the field officers knew me, I having been often in Dublin with the Government when King James was there, and would discourse familiarly. I asked them what had I done that they kept me prisoner in that sad condition, and did not bring me to a trial. Colonel Moore said they had nothing against me, but they understood I was a very witty man, and capable to do them an injury, and that was the reason they kept me. I told them that was poor justice, to punish a man for what he was capable of doing, and not for what he had done.

" The next day John Clibborn came again with victuals, but we could get no straw, and I was much spent and my spirit grieved with their wicked company, so that I desired to die quietly in a dungeon rather than be among them. I sent John Clibborn to the Governor to say I desired to be put on trial or be removed to prison. Colonel Grace said he was sorry for me, and they were none of them my enemies but the Dunns, who were all rogues, and he durst not release me, for many eyes were upon him, because he was kind to the English; but to send me to the dungeon he could not find in his heart to do it. The town was so throng of people that there was no room, that I could be easy in, to be had, so he was in a strait, and knew not what to do for me. So John Clibborn requested to let me go with him to his house at the Moate, and he would engage his life, body, and all he had for my true imprisonment, and that I would come when he sent for me alive or dead. The Governor let me go with him; thus the Lord provided in the time of my great distress.

"When I came to the Moate, with much difficulty I got a few lines writ and sent to my wife, which was a great satisfaction to her and Friends, who were under great trouble of mind.

"One of my sons who was with me had a tan-yard well stocked with hides and leather, and about a week after our house was burned my wife went to fetch them off, with some English neighbours and carts to help, but while loading them, Lieutenant Richard Dunn, with a multitude of Raparees came upon them; they were forced to run for their lives and leave all to the Raparees. But my wife not being able to outrun them, they took and stript her naked, it being cold weather and she being ancient, and having to go thus two miles, got a surfeit of cold which continued with her till she died about seven months after.

" The next morning a small party of English soldiers fell upon that great company and killed the said Richard Dunn, so he was prevented from burning Mountmellick as he had threatened to do.

" While I was at the Moate many of the Irish came daily to get what they could carry off, there came also Colonel Bourke, with 300 firelocks, as a Frontier, to intercept the English soldiers. He was very loving, and promised that when he got to Athlone I should have my liberty. So, with his assistance, the Governor set me at liberty, having let my two sons go three or four days before, who were gone to their mother. So, being set at liberty, I got to Streamstown, the next English garrison, though it was difficult and dangerous travelling, there being now little but killing and destruction on both sides.

" I next got to Mullingar, a great garrison of the English, where the officers and soldiers were very glad to see me. Several of them had sworn that if they had killed me and my sons, they would have killed all the Irish they met with.

" Going on to Mountmellick I met my wife ; we shifted for house room as well as we could, the town being thronged with soldiers and families driven from their homes in the country, many of whom died from want of necessaries and with grief for their losses. Now the Irish preyed much abroad in the country to destroy it, so that the English army marched out to drive them back over the Shannon. Major Kirk came with part of his army to Mountmellick, to settle garrisons about, to save the country. He would have me to go with him to Rosenallis, and shew him the place, so being commanded, I went with him. Many Irish there under English protection supposed I had occasioned Major

Kirk's coming to make a garrison there, and were very angry with me, for this would hinder them harbouring the Raparees, as they had frequently done before, wherefore they got eight or nine bloody Raparees to lie in wait to kill me. They then tried twice to get me to return to Rosenallis, professing great friendship, saying the soldiers were pulling down my out-houses which remained unburned, but I was restrained by that Hand that knew their evil design, and would not let me fall into their snare. Next morning John Dobson with his son and cousin going that way, were barbarously murdered.

"Now as soon as the ways were open to travel I went with some Friends to the north, as we went by Dundalk, where the armies had been in conflict, many bones lay around, and tufts of grass growing out of the carcasses of men as if it had been from heaps of manure. I told Friends who were with me, 'You may remember I declared in public in years past, in many places, that the Lord would spread the carcasses of men as dung on the face of the earth, and you now see it this day.'

LURGAN MEETING-HOUSE.   FIRST IN IRELAND.   BUILT BY WILLIAM EDMUNDSON.

" In that journey I had many sweet, comfortable meetings, Friends' hearts were glad, and we were greatly refreshed in the Lord Jesus."

William Edmundson continued for twenty-five years after this time of war and famine to fill his place as a minister of the Gospel and a patriot in his adopted country. He saw tranquillity restored under the Government of William and Mary, and travelled in his Master's service until a year before his death, passing away in 1712, in the eighty-sixth year of his age. From his papers we make the following extract: " Our Saviour left us an example, when under the sense of drinking that cup of suffering for the sins of all mankind, and to offer to God that great offering for their ransom, He prayed: ' Father, if Thou be willing, remove this cup from me, nevertheless not my will, but Thine be done.'

" I am now clear of the world and the things of it. I see not anything I have left undone, which the Lord required of me. Heaven and earth, sea and dry land, and all things shall be shaken, nothing shall stand but what is according to the will of God."

In one of his last records he says : "I am content to rest in the will of God, Who has lengthened my days to old age, and done great things for me, to Whose great and worthy Name be glory and honour, for ever and ever more." Amen.

CHAPTER II.

THOMAS WILSON.

About the year 1655, six generations back from the busy world of to-day, Thomas Wilson was born in Soulby, Cumberland. With a short sketch of his life we begin these family memorials.

His name, unrecorded in the annals of the great in this world, is doubtless numbered among those who have fought the good fight in the Army of the Lamb. Following his Captain through suffering, danger and opposition, he preached the Gospel freely, became wise in storming the Kingdom of Darkness, and instrumental in turning many to righteousness—one of those who shall "shine like the stars for ever and ever."

The political and religious state of society was, in England as well as in Ireland, one of disturbance and upheaval. "Some time before this the Church of England, as a Protestant Church, had been established, and many who were dissatisfied with the settlement of it, had formed themselves into different sects. A great number of persons in the Kingdom, approving neither of the religion of the Establishment nor of the other denominations alluded to, withdrew from the communion of every outward church; nor had the Reformation taken place so long but that thousands were still very ignorant."* The spirit of earnest enquiry, the seeking after God which at this time manifested itself, was the effect of a visitation of divine love to meet the need of the period. Formality and deadness largely prevailed in professing churches. Countless numbers failed to find help and enlightenment from man and turned to God himself to satisfy the hunger of

---

* Clarkson's Portraiture of Friends

the soul, and thus, in the language of an old writer : " Groaning seekers became in time joyful finders," by the revelation of God through Jesus Christ.*

As we have seen in the former chapter, many of these joyful finders instead of returning to the worship in their own churches formed themselves into little gatherings, to wait upon, and worship God in spirit and in truth. They did not intend to create a division, or a sect, but called themselves " Friends of God and Mankind." From among these earnest souls many were called to go forth and testify to the people the things they had seen and handled of the Word of Life. But soon persecution, bitter even unto death, broke up their meetings and dragged the most prominent to filthy crowded prisons, where they lay for years, and where the sufferings of many were ended only by death. But nothing could check their devotion, and when there failed men and women to sustain the public worship, youths and children continued in some places to

---

* See Appendix A.

gather amid the ruins of their Meeting-houses.

In the space of three years 10,000 had joined the Friends in the City of London, chiefly through the preaching of Francis Howgel, and Edward Barrows. The former died in Appleby Jail in 1668; the latter in Newgate in 1661, after ten years of faithful ministry in the highways and hedges, in the lanes and streets of the cities.

"In the time of our first acquaintance," writes a friend of his youth, "Thomas Wilson was light and airy in conversation, much given to sporting and jesting, having a desire to make people laugh and be merry, as he then called it. But when the Lord was pleased to visit him, and break his rest, giving a sense of this vanity and unprofitable life, a great change was wrought, and all his mirth was turned into mourning. Solitary places became his resort, and a deep concern to seek a Saviour rested on him." This continued until, as another of his friends remarked, "It pleased the Lord to reveal His Son in him and give him an understanding what to do." And here

Thomas Wilson's own simple story of his life and travels may be taken up.

" My parents, Edward and Anne Wilson, brought me up in the profession of the Church of England. While yet a youth I had great hungering and thirsting after the living God and His Son, Jesus Christ, and went with great diligence to hear the priests, and carefully minded what was spoken. When I heard of one noted as a good man, and who preached two sermons in a day, I went from our own parish, after the forenoon service, eight miles on foot to hear the afternoon sermon.

" But the more I sought to hear the more my hunger and thirst increased, and in times of singing psalms a thoughtfulness came into my heart that men should be made holy before they could rightly sing to the praise and glory of God. Secret cries and humble prayers ascended to the living Lord God of heaven and earth for a knowledge of the way of salvation, but being in the wilderness of men's creeds and forms I could find no peace of conscience.

" Thus I continued in great sorrow, being weary of the heavy load of sin.

" Yet many texts of Scripture were opened to my understanding, and I began to see what was not of faith was sin, even in worship and service of the Great God, and I remembered the words of our blessed Lord and Saviour, ' This people draweth near to me with their mouth and honoureth me with their lips, but their heart is far from me.' And also that our heavenly Saviour had said at Jacob's Well : ' The hour cometh, and now is, that the true worshippers shall worship the Father in spirit and in truth, for the Father seeketh such to worship Him.' This worship in the renewings of the Holy Ghost and not in the oldness of the letter I longed to know, but could not find it, neither could any priest I conversed with tell me how or where to find it.

" About this time I attended an evening meeting of the people called ' Quakers,' with strong desires if it was the true way I might have some testimony thereof by the blessed Word in my own heart. After some time of silence a Friend began to speak, directing me to a waiting upon the Lord by faith to receive from Him power over every unclean thought,

E

by which heavenly power men might glorify
and praise the holy Name of the Lord.

" I felt my soul much in love therewith ; and
smiting upon my breast, said in my heart,
this is what I greatly wanted—power against
every vain thought and idle word.   The Lord's
power arose in the meeting, and fell mightily
upon me, to the breaking and tendering of my
heart ; and a glorious time it was, as the
mighty day of the Lord ; so that great fear,
trembling and shaking seized me, insomuch
that the table whereon I leaned and Friends
sat, was shaken.   Thus being sensible in
some measure of the glorious name and power
of the Lord Jesus, I was full of inward cries
to this effect : ' O Lord ! create in me a clean
heart ' ; for I saw the old one was not clean,
and that I had been kissing the letter but not
the Son, as advised by the Holy Scripture,
which saith : ' Kiss the Son, lest He be
angry,' &c.

" And now was a time of the Lord's fierce
anger because of sin, He having shewed me
all things that ever I had done, and condemned
the evil ; so I was made willing to love and

dwell under His righteous judgments. It was upon my mind, that I must cease from all the doctrines of men, will-worship, hearing the priests, and repeating their sermons, which I had delighted in, and was in the practice of as religious duties, and sit down among Friends in their silent meetings, to wait upon the Lord for His heavenly teachings and holy leadings ; in the performance of which inward and heavenly worship, the great power of God did wonderfully break in among us, and many young people turned to the Lord with all their hearts.

" So the Friends in our meeting became very tender and heavenly minded, and had great love one towards another ; the heart-melting power of God being much felt, even when no words were spoken, so that we experienced Christ to dwell in our hearts by faith,* and the

---

* Before the magistrates in Derby, George Fox was examined from one o'clock till nine at night. " At last," he says, " they asked whether I was sanctified ?   I answered yes, for I was in the Paradise of God, then they asked if I had no sin ?   I said Christ my Saviour had taken away my sin, in Him is no sin   They asked how we knew that Christ did abide in us.   I answered by His Spirit that he had given us—they temptingly asked if any of us were Christ ?   I answered nay, *we are nothing*, Christ is all.   So when they had wearied themselves in examining me, they committed me to the House of Correction, as blasphemer, for six months "

E 2

renewings of the Holy Ghost were shed on our souls abundantly, whereby some were so filled that they were concerned to declare the things of the kingdom, and to tell what God had done for their souls."

And now, having been delivered from form and shadow and made a possessor of the eternal substance—Christ within, the hope of glory—Thomas Wilson goes on to say: " One of the first that came forth in prayer and supplication was William Greenup, and I was the next in a testimony for the Lord, which was in much fear and trembling, yet the Word of the Lord in and through me was as a devouring fire, burning against all sin and iniquity ; and the Lord made us cry aloud to turn people from all vain worships to the living God, who is a Holy Spirit.

" The precious life of Jesus broke in wonderfully amongst us, so that we felt drawings to visit other meetings in the country, wherein the Lord's heavenly power was plentifully enjoyed.

" In the year 1682, it was upon me from the Lord, in a divine opening, to visit Friends in some parts of Ireland. I took shipping at Workington, and landed at Dublin, where I was altogether a stranger. After I had attended a meeting, Friends inquired which way I intended to go ; I told them I had a desire to go to see some Friends that dwelt between the west and north ; a Friend answered he thought there was no such place inhabited by Friends (or to that effect), but if I would see Friends, I must go north or south. This brought great trouble upon my mind, and I became very low in spirit, questioning in myself whether I was not mistaken in that which I thought was the Lord's powerful opening in my heart, shewing me both the place and people, and wherein I thought I had the mind of Christ in the holy vision of life ; and the cries of my heart were great unto the Lord in secret, why I was mistaken ; but after some time, a living hope sprung in me that I was not mistaken, and that the Friends lay or inhabited as I had seen.

" A Friend, named Abraham Fuller, spoke kindly to me, and said he lived near the middle of Ireland, and if I would go with him we might get a meeting amongst Friends at Edenderry; and in the way I had much peace in going with him. We had a blessed meeting with Friends at Edenderry, and next day, travelling towards Lehinche, where he dwelt, he asked me if I understood the compass, I told him no, and that I had not seen any compass in all my lifetime but that in the ship wherein I came to Dublin. He was then very cheerful, and lovingly said he remembered that I had said in Dublin I would go between the west and north, ' Which now,' said he, ' I see is true, for we go even as thou then said '; at which I was truly thankful to the Lord, who never fails to be gracious, and His blessed Word is infallible. For then I, like Samuel, knew it was the Word of the Lord that called me into His work and service, and shewed me these things before I went from home. . . . . .

" This Province Meeting was large, and divers able Friends in the ministry were there ; but I was very low in my mind, and did not go up into the gallery but sat down a little within the door. Many people came in, so that the place about where I sat was much thronged, and it being a time that the rabble sort of people were very rude, several such were there that day.

" I being under great exercise of spirit, the powerful Word of the Lord filled my heart; so I rose and preached the Gospel in the demonstration of the spirit and power that was upon me. The rabble were astonished and became very quiet, and the Lord's heavenly power did shine forth gloriously, and under a weighty sense thereof the meeting concluded.

" This brought me into acquaintance with Friends unto whom I had been a stranger. I understood, afterwards, they were sore afraid when I stood up ' that my appearance ' (*i.e.* the words he spoke) ' would have been hurtful.'

" After this meeting I went into County Wicklow and had heavenly-blessed meetings among a lowly, plain people. Soon the motion of life for travelling ceased, and I durst go no further.

" In a little time came James Dickinson, a young man from Cumberland, to visit Friends, and the Lord was pleased to open my way to go with him, we, being young, travelled together in true brotherly love, great humility, and godly fear; and the blessed heavenly power of the Lord did often tender our hearts in meetings, as also the hearts of many Friends, and we had a prosperous journey in the will of God. So I saw it was good to wait the Lord's time in all things; and having travelled through Leinster and Munster, James Dickinson went northward, but I was afraid of running before my true Guide, because they who run, and are not sent of God, can neither profit the people nor themselves. So I staid at work in the City of Waterford about sixteen weeks, and went from thence to Dublin, and staid the Half-year's Meeting there, which was large and very good; then took shipping and landed at Liverpool, with my former companion, James Dickinson; and though it was now a time of great persecution of Friends in England, it pleased the Lord to give us a peaceable and prosperous journey through the meetings of Friends all along in our way to Cumberland.

" In a little time after, I, with my dear companion James Dickinson, visited Friends in the two counties of Cumberland and West-moreland. At Kendal some persons came to break up our meeting, and began to pull out Friends, and, in a very rude manner, took out my companion. Then the Word of the Lord came mightily upon me, and I was made bold to stand up and preach the Everlasting Gospel amongst them. The holy power of the Lord came mightily over the hearts of Friends, and even the opposers were made quiet a considerable time ; but after I had stood about an hour, they came and pulled me to the door. I asked for my hat, and they said: 'Give him his hat, he does well to put it off when he preaches.' And after they had asked me many questions, I asked one of them whether he was a believer in Jesus Christ or not ? He said: 'Yes, and in the Apostles' Doctrine ' ; then I told him he never read that *they* disturbed any religious assembly, except Paul, before he knew the Lord Jesus, so I sat me down and all being very still, James Dickinson kneeled down in prayer, and the Lord's heavenly power came over all, and the meeting ended very quietly.

"In 1684 I and my companion had many blessed meetings in North and South Wales. At Redstone an informer laid violent hands on me while preaching the Word of God to the people. I spoke to him mildly. He sat down, with the constable and the men who came in their company, and I preached the way of salvation to them all. After which James Dickinson kneeled in prayer, when the informer came to pull him off his knees, but could not, he being fervent in prayer to the Lord. The meeting ended well, thanksgiving be unto Him for ever and ever. Amen.

"The informer laid hands on me next. I asked for his warrant; he answered he was an officer, and that I had nothing to do to ask him for a warrant. Friends told him it was but a civil question, so we fell into some friendly discourse. I was very pleasant and easy in spirit; and walking to and fro in discourse, one of the company said I smiled (which they admired, we being likely to go to prison). I answered: ' That I came in the true love of the Lord Jesus Christ to visit them, and had nothing but love and good-will to them all,' and turning to the informer, said to him : ' If thou was in a journey, as we are, and any man should ask thee to go with him before a justice of the peace, without the king's justice's warrant, thou would think it below thee, as a man, to go so.' This being mildly spoken to him, he gave a sudden answer, saying : ' To be sure I would.' ' Then,' said I, ' consider our case '; whereupon, perceiving he had over-shot himself, he rode away and left us.

" We having appointed a meeting to be next day at Haverfordwest, went thither that night, and next morning to the meeting, wherein after a little time the glorious power of the Lord did shine, and that text of Holy Scripture was opened : ' We shall not find any occasion against this Daniel, except we find it against him concerning the law of his God.' —Dan. vi, 5. And it was further remarked that after they had prevailed with King Darius to sign a decree, whereby Daniel might be ensnared in performing his duty unto his God, this righteous man declined not his duty through fear of suffering, but was very bold as well as innocent, as appears in the tenth verse of the

same chapter, viz., ' Now when Daniel knew
that the writing was signed, he went into his
house ; and his windows being open in his
chamber toward Jerusalem, he kneeled upon
his knees three times a day, and prayed, and
gave thanks before his God, as he did afore-
time.' This subject was preached to the people,
as our case ; men having nothing against us,
but for worshipping the Lord God of Daniel in
His Holy Spirit, according to the institution of
of our blessed Lord and Saviour above sixteen
hundred years ago ; and that in this glorious
Gospel time, we are to be very diligent and
faithful to the Lord, to keep up our religious
meetings, even in stormy times of persecution,
referring to that of Daniel, who was blessed of
the Lord for his faithfulness ; boldly declaring
and affirming that the Lord, whom we serve
in the Gospel of His Son, will reward all His
faithful children and people ; instancing many
proofs out of the Holy Scriptures.   The aforesaid informer, and several priests, whereof
his brother was one, together with some of the
town-officers, being at the outside of the house
and hearing these Gospel truths preached,

were very sober, and staid a great while. Then some of them said: ' Let us pull them out of their meeting '; but others said: ' No, by no means, for if this be the Quakers' doctrine, it is good and sound, we never heard the like, let them alone.' So our meeting ended in prayer and thanksgiving to the great Lord of heaven and earth, who is worthy for ever and ever.

" This informer fined Friends very much; but the Lord, by one means or another, prevented their goods from being taken away, and, lastly, by the death of King Charles the Second. After this, no informer troubled us, though we had many meetings to visit, in all which we had blessed, sweet waterings, and a confirming ministry; and Friends were glad in that the God of Peace had rebuked the storm.

" Friends at Great Strickland, not being suffered to meet at their usual meeting-place, met in the highway before the meeting-house door; and the officers came when I was preaching the Word of the Lord, but were very sober, and did not break up our meeting.

From thence I came home, where my mother and family, with Friends and neighbours, were very glad to see me safe returned, in that stormy time.

" After some stay at my outward employ about home, I found drawings to visit Friends in Northumberland, Durham and Yorkshire, and had many blessed meetings, mostly peaceable, though the storm of persecution was not yet fully ended. I went into Warwickshire, Oxfordshire, and Oxford City, where I heard the scholars had been rude, and much abused Friends. I went into that city on a First-day morning, in great fear and humility, being a stranger to all Friends there, and sat me down in a corner of the meeting-house. Friends sat by the sides of the house, and left the middle empty for the rabble (as I thought). We having sat a little time, a Friend began to speak, and had spoken but a very few words before the scholars came in, in such abundance, that they filled the middle part of the house. The Friend sat down as soon as they came in, and the meeting being in silence, they began to talk one to another, and spy out who would preach; and seeing me like a traveller, said : ' That in the corner,' looking rudely upon me ; and thus talking one to another for some time. The Word of the Lord was strong in my heart to preach unto them. But I was first to say : ' Sit down, young men, we shall be glad of your company so long as you are civil ' ; then they all sat down, and began to listen earnestly. I preached the way to the kingdom of heaven, to be in Jesus Christ, regeneration, to be born again ; and that the blessed Jesus taught this doctrine to Nicodemus : ' Except a man be born again, he cannot see the kingdom of God.'—John iii, 3. And though he was a master or teacher in Israel, yet being carnally-minded, he could not understand these things ; neither can any carnally-minded men now know the things of God, ' For no man knoweth the Father but the Son, and he to whomsoever the Son will reveal Him.' So those that preach against revelation, they preach against the true knowledge of the living God and life eternal ; for our blessed Lord said : ' This is life eternal, that they might know Thee, the only true God, and Jesus Christ whom Thou hast sent.' And so I went on in preaching as it opened in me. The scholars went away quietly, and the meeting ended in prayer to Almighty God.*

"I went from Oxford to High Wycombe, and so to the City of London, where I staid some time, and had many blessed meetings amongst Friends; several of which meetings were held in the streets, where Friends were kept out of their meeting-houses, and the

---

* Of another visit to Oxford, a companion, Thomas Storey, writes: "At Oxford we had a comfortable meeting, for though many of the collegians were there, who used to be rude in an extraordinary manner, yet the invisible power of the Word of Life being over them at that time, they were quiet under the authoritative ministry of Thomas Wilson. Many of them were struck with amazement and surprise, and their eyes were filled with tears, so that several of the elder sort retired, but in a decent manner, as if to hide the effect of Truth, which, if they had staid, could not have been concealed ; but above all the rest, a young man, a very comely youth, who, by his appearance and behaviour, seemed to be the son of some noble person, was most deeply affected The Lord gave us glorious times on our way to Bristol. The sensible enjoyment of His divine and soul-melting presence, to our general and mutual consolation (for in those days Friends were near the Lord, and one another in Him) : the canopy of His love was over us, and we rejoiced together therein, but with holy fear and with trembling, and had often occasion to say concerning the way of the Lord, as of old, and with respect to His noble servant (T. W.), that 'He maketh His angels spirits, and His ministers a flame of fire,' for so *he* was indeed, in an eminent manner to the churches where he came in this visit, as generally elsewhere at other times."

Lord's Holy Word was preached boldly in the streets of that city.

" In London I met with my dear companion James Dickinson, and was exceeding glad to see him. We both having had a great exercise in our minds to visit the Lord's people in America, and having certificates on that account from the respective Monthly Meetings we belonged unto, we laid our intentions before Friends in London for their concurrence ; which they received very kindly, and approved of, believing that the Lord had called us to preach His gospel in that part of the world. But the times seemed like to be very dangerous and stormy : the French being at war against England, had a great fleet at sea ; and while we were in London, the rumour was, that the French fleet lay about thirty or forty leagues from the Land's End, in the way we should pass. This brought a very great concern upon us, with many inward seekings and supplications to the Lord, if it was His blessed will, that He might be pleased to preserve us. And being strong in faith, that it was easy with the Lord God to deliver us, we trusted

F

in His holy power; and I being in deep travail of soul, had an opening from the Lord, that it was His holy will to deliver us, and we should live to see it; which I believed, and was humbly thankful to the Lord, and told my dear companion thereof with great joy; for we being nearly united in true love, could freely open our minds each to the other. He also told me, 'that being under a travail of soul, the Lord had shewed him, *That the French fleet would encompass us on both sides, and also behind, and come very near; but the Lord would send in a great mist and darkness between us and them, in which we should sail away, and see them no more.*' Thus we imparted our minds to each other before we left London; and our openings so agreeing one with another, we were the more confirmed that it was of the Lord. We staid in the City till the Yearly Meeting, 1691, was over: a blessed meeting it was, and Friends' tender love was towards us, many ancient Friends were there; particularly William Edmundson from Ireland, who gave us tender advice, which we took very kindly, he having been in America in Truth's service.

" We sailed from London to Gravesend, and had a blessed meeting with the Friends that accompanied us from the City, and after meeting, took leave of each other. We sailed from thence to the Downs, and the master being very kind, we went on shore, and had some meetings thereabout, wherein the Lord's holy power tendered our hearts together. From thence we sailed to Plymouth, where we had some blessed, comfortable meetings, and Friends were very glad to see us.

" On the 9th day of Fifth Month, 1691, we went aboard, and sailed to Falmouth, where all the fleet put in. After sailing forth we met with the French fleet, who gave us chase, coming up, under English colours, within musket shot of us : then the English putting up their own colours, the French began to fire at them. The first French ship that came up was very large, and it was said to have ninety guns ; nigh unto which ship were eleven more, and seventy sail behind them, as some of our company said they counted. The first ship pursued us, and fired hard, a broadside at every time ; and being come up within musket-shot, the Lord was graciously pleased to hear our prayers, and sent a great mist, with thick darkness, which interposed between us and them, so that they could not see us, nor we them, any more. Then James Dickinson arose from his seat, and took me by the hand, saying : ' Now I hope the Lord will deliver us '; for he had seen all fulfilled, which the Lord had shewed before we left London. This was cause of great gladness to me, who had been under a deep travail of spirit with fasting and prayer to the Lord, that He who smote His enemies in times past with blindness, might please to do so now ; which the Lord did please to answer, whereof our hearts were truly thankful to him. My fasting, praying, and inward giving of thanks continued three days.

" Two ships of our company that escaped, came up with us, which we were glad to see ; and the captain of our vessel, being a very kind man, called to those in the other two ships to come aboard his, and have a meeting with us ; which they readily did ; and a large and good meeting we had, giving glory to the

Lord's holy name for His great deliverance. So we sailed on our way rejoicing, continuing healthy and well until we landed at Barbadoes, which was on the 24th of the Sixth Month, 1691. Here we found a great sickness amongst the people, but Friends were glad to see us. The first meeting we had there, was at the burial of a noted Friend, where we sounded forth the Word of the Lord, a multitude of people being there, both white and black; the Lord's Holy Word powerfully reached, and broke many of their hearts into great tenderness : the blacks stood astonished, with tears running down their cheeks and naked breasts. We staid above two months in that island, in all which time the sickness raged ; yet we had many large and precious meetings, to which there was great flocking, the people being very much humbled by the sickness. So being clear in our spirits of that island, we parted with Friends in great love and sweetness.

" On the 22nd of the Eighth Month, we took shipping for New York, and arrived there the 23rd of the Ninth Month, being about a month's time ; and though we had a great storm in our passage, which lasted ten days, the Lord's good hand preserved us. But the captain was very much down in his mind and under indisposition of body, in the time of our voyage, and said to me : 'We' (meaning himself and the crew) 'should die like rotten sheep.' I said: ' No, captain, do not fear '—for I saw that the ship would go safe in ; and after some further discourse he hugged me in his arms and seemed to rejoice. We accordingly arrived at New York, and had a meeting there, and from thence went to Long Island, where we had several good meetings with Friends. Then the Word of the Lord was in me, thus : ' Hasten, hasten, to visit My great people in Philadelphia '; so we went forward, having some good meetings in our way thither.

" When we came to Philadelphia there was a great division raised amongst Friends by George Keith. We preached the Lord Jesus powerfully amongst them, and had some labour tending to peace. My companion had it often upon him to warn them all *to keep more inward to the Lord*. We staid some time there, visiting Friends in that province, and had many precious meetings amongst them ; some of which were kept without doors, for want of room, as there were great flockings to hear the Truth declared, although it was Winter time. We went from thence into Maryland, and visited Friends on the eastern and western shores Then we travelled to Virginia, the Lord's good presence accompanying us from time to time, and we found a tender, humble people there.

"We went from Virginia towards North Carolina, where the floods were so great that we could not travel on horseback, but waded barefoot through swamps and waters. Friends and other people were exceedingly glad to see us, they not having had any visit by a travelling Friend of the Ministry for several years. We had good service amongst them ; for the Lord's heavenly power wonderfully supported us under our difficulties and hard travel, the country being so full of wild creatures, that wolves would come and roar about the houses in the night. So after having had many good and heavenly meetings with Friends there we took leave of them, and returned through the wilderness to Virginia, then travelled up James River, having service as we went, until we came to Curles, where we had some meetings to satisfaction amongst Friends and other people.

"We went from Curles through the woods to Black Creek, where we had appointed a meeting; and, none having been there before, the Sheriff with some officers came to break it up. James Dickinson being then declaring, the Sheriff asked him: 'From whom he had his commission to preach?' James answered to this effect: 'I have my commission from the great God, unto whom thou and I must give an account.' At these words the Sheriff seemed much astonished; and after they had had some further discourse, the Sheriff swore; for which James reproved him. He answered: 'I know I should not swear,' seeming then very mild, and said: 'We had a gracious king and queen, and they had given us our liberty.' I then stood up and asked the Sheriff: 'As he had said that we had a gracious king and queen, that had given us our liberty' (which was true), 'then by what law would the Sheriff persecute us?' He then turned about and went away. Whereupon James Dickinson spake aloud, saying: 'Let the Sheriff answer the question'; but he took the man of the house with him, and then sent him back to bid us go off his land. I said: 'We did not come there without his leave, and both he and the people might know we had not broken the king's law, and if they would have a little patience, and hear what we had to say for the Lord, we would go peaceably away.' Most of the people staid, and we had a heavenly meeting amongst them. Several were convinced, and in a short time after a Meeting-house was built, and a Meeting settled, which I think is kept there still.

"After the said meeting at Black Creek, one Charles Fleming, who had not been at any of our meetings before, being reached by the Truth, kindly invited us to lodge with him, which we did. From his house we travelled towards Maryland, having company a little way of the first day's journey, and then were left in the woods; after having travelled all day, we sat down in the dusk of the evening, to eat a little bread and cheese. My mare went out of my hand, and in a little time I perceived she had found water, at which I was very glad; and I think I never drank anything more sweet and pleasant to me, than that water was.

"We lodged that night in the woods, and as soon as the day brake set forward on our journey through the woods, northward; and as we were travelling, met with two men, one of whom being an ancient, comely man, kindly invited us to his house, where we staid two nights and had a meeting, though he was an elder among the Presbyterians; he also lent us his boat to go over Potomack River. The next night we lodged at a poor man's house, and had no bed to lie in. As we were sitting by his fire, he told us that George Fox and John Burnyeat had travelled in those parts, and had meetings on both sides of the river, and many were convinced, but several of them fell away. We got next day over Patuxent River, into Maryland, and had many blessed meetings amongst Friends on both sides of the bay.

" Now leaving Friends at Philadelphia, we went into the country to a meeting, to which George Keith came: he asked me where we would be on the First-day, saying also, that he had appointed a meeting to be next First-day at Crosswicks; and finding freedom, I went thither: but my companion, James Dickinson, found drawings from the Lord to go to Philadelphia, and be at the meeting there that First-day. Thither George Keith came, fawningly, as though he and James Dickinson were in unity. But after he had done, James stood up in great authority in the Lord's power, and confuted George's doctrine and practice, setting Truth over him and his party, and opened the mystery of salvation to the people to their great satisfaction.

"After this George Keith went away in great wrath, and the people who were not Friends, being many, cried aloud : ' Give way and let the devil come out, for the little black man from England has got the day.' "

With regard to this mention of George Keith, it may be stated, he was a man of position and education, who embraced the views of Friends, and accompanied Fox and Penn to Holland as an authorized minister. A few years later, however, he became very troublesome, and soon after Fox's death the Society was harassed and embittered through the schism caused by Keith's defection. He visited Pennsylvania, hoping to sow discord there. Sewell remarks : " He was a very witty person, and esteemed very learned." He accused Friends of saying the Light within was sufficient without anything else for Salvation ; from whence he endeavoured to prove that they excluded Christ Jesus as not necessary to Salvation. " But they," says Sewell, " denied this to be their doctrine." During the Yearly Meeting in London, 1694, Keith behaved so violently that the Friends considered it needful to disavow all connection with him by sending the following declaration of their faith to Parliament :—

" Be it known unto all that we sincerely believe and confess—

 1st. That Jesus of Nazareth, who was born of the Virgin Mary, is the true Messiah, the very Christ, the Son of the living God, to whom all the prophets gave

witness, and that we do highly value His death, sufferings, works, offices, and merits for the redemption of mankind, together with His laws, doctrines, and ministry.

2nd. That this very Christ of God, who is the Lamb of God that taketh away the sin of the world, was slain, was dead, and is alive, and lives for ever in His divine eternal glory, dominion, and power with the Father.

3rd. That the Holy Scriptures of the Old and New Testament are of divine authority, as being given by inspiration of God.

4th. That the magistry or civil government is God's ordinance, the good end thereof being for the punishment of evil doers, and praise of them that do well." *

Keith next conformed to the Established Church, and was ordained, after which he was sent by the Bishops to America to oppose the

* Sewell's " History of Friends " Ed 1832, p 258

Quakers and gain adherents.   On his return a living was presented to him near Shoreham, but so poor a one, that he was obliged to sell his library for £10.

One writer affirms that his life and death was pious and exemplary.   Another says that on his death-bed he was heard to remark : " I wish I had died when I was a Quaker, for then I am sure it would have been well with my soul." *

" On the 17th of the Sixth Month, 1692, we took shipping at Boston, for Barbadoes, and after we had been about two or three days at sea, the ship, being new, sprung a leak ; part of our lading being tar, it ran out of the barrels into the hold, and our pumps clogged, so things looked very dangerous.   I stripped myself to work at the pump, and James went with the captain to search the hold, where they found a treenail hole that the carpenter had left unfilled, and after they had got it stopped, through the Lord's great mercy we arrived safe at Barbadoes.   Some time before we went

---

* Bickley's " Life of George Fox."

in, it fell thick, dark weather, continuing so all the forenoon ; but about twelve o'clock the sun broke out, and our sailors got an observation ; immediately after which, the mist struck in again, and the darkness was so great that although there was a privateer which had laid several days in that latitude, we escaped her, and got well in. So that we saw the same Hand which preserved us in our first going there, by bringing in a thick mist, had again preserved us in like manner, a second time ; which was cause of great joy to us and Friends on the island, who gladly received us.

" We landed at Barbadoes on the 2nd day of the Eighth Month, 1692, where we staid some time, and visited Friends' Meetings thoroughly, and had good service for the Lord ; the sickness which was in the island at our first coming still continuing, whereby the people were very much humbled ; and their exercise was further increased by a plot the blacks had laid to murder the white people, which was discovered in manner following :

" A certain man having a black servant, whom he respected, called him in and gave him a dram ; wherewith he was so well pleased that upon his going out he said to himself : ‘ My master is a very good man, great pity to kill my master ’ ; and being overheard, information was carried to his master ; upon which he had him apprehended, and examined before the Governor. He confessed the whole plot, which was : ‘ To kill all the white men on Sunday night, and to seize the fort, shipping, horses, and arms.’   But being thus discovered, many of the blacks were taken and hung up in gibbets alive till they died.

“ Being clear of Barbadoes, we went from thence to Antigua, where we staid some time, and had several large meetings amongst the people ; the Lord’s power did so prevail over them that several were convinced of the Truth, and afterwards became faithful Friends.

“ We passed from Antigua to the Island of Nevis ; and when near it had a consultation whether to go in on the north or south side thereof ; and by the favourable direction of Divine Providence for our preservation, we went in on the south side, where we heard that a French privateer, that lay on the north side of the island, had taken a vessel about the same time. We staid several weeks in that island, and had good service for the Lord. Many of the inhabitants had been visited with a mortal distemper, of which many were taken away. There had been four priests on the island before, but when we came, there was but one of them living : he was a great drunkard and swearer ; when the inhabitants came to our meetings, and were so reached by the Lord's power, that they confessed to the Truth, this wicked priest was very angry, and told them he would come and dispute with us on the First-day. This being spread through the island, many of the inhabitants of great note came to the meeting, though the priest did not come, but went to the Governor to inform him against us. We had a large meeting, in which the Everlasting Gospel was proclaimed amongst them, and all were warned to repent of their sins, and turn to the light of Jesus Christ. Many hearts were reached ; one that was a justice of the peace confessed to the Truth, and wrote to the Governor on our behalf.

G

" Now being clear of this island, our names were put up at a public place, as notice of our going off the island, and certificates written and carried by a Friend to the Governor to be signed by him—but he would not, for he had been much enraged by the priest, and threatened that he would put us in the fort.   So we took horses and went with the master of the ship, with whom we had taken our passage, to the Governor's house.   He appeared very angry with us, and said: ' We were spies, come to spy out the strength of the island.'   We told him : ' We were no spies, but true men,' and to satisfy the Governor we shewed him a pass that had the Secretary's seal on it, which we had at our coming out of England, whereupon all governors and officers were commanded to let us pass.   When he saw the broad seal his countenance fell, and he asked why we had not shewed it him before ? We replied : 'We had not shewed it then, but for his satisfaction that we were not spies,' and further told him: ' We came in the love of God to visit our Friends and the inhabitants of the island.'   Then he signed the certificate, and called for a bottle of wine to drink with the captain and us, but we would not drink any with him. We were deeply bowed under the sense of God's goodness to us, who had not only drawn us into His service, but made way for us, and wrought our deliverance. In the latitude of Bermudas a tornado came, which is a gust of storm (our top sails being a-trip), and laid the vessel on one side like a log of wood, and it remained so for some time; in which time the glory of the Lord did so shine upon us, that the fear of death was taken away, and our hearts were filled with the joy of God's salvation.

" Now being clear of our service for the Lord in America, we took shipping from Nevis homeward, and in about six weeks landed in the Highlands of Scotland. We travelled from thence by land into Cumberland, where Friends greatly rejoiced at seeing us, they having heard that we were taken by the French. From hence we travelled up to the Yearly Meeting at London, having some meetings in our way thither : we had a very blessed Yearly Meeting, Friends being in

G 2

great love and unity, and greatly rejoiced to see us, as we did to see them; and there is great thankfulness in my soul to the Lord, for His manifold favours and preservation, both by sea and land.

CHAPTER III.

THOMAS WILSON IN IRELAND.

"In the Autumn of 1695 I married Mary, daughter of Thomas Bewley, of Wood Hall, Cumberland, who proved a true helpmeet indeed to me. Soon after our marriage I found freedom to remove with my wife and her brother into Ireland, and we settled near Edenderry in the King's County." To this place, on Thomas Wilson's first visit to Ireland, he believed he was called—"Somewhere between the west and north." Here he continued to reside until his death in his own house at Thornwell, a property still in the possession of his descendants.

The Journal of Thomas Wilson proceeds:

" Some time after my removal to Ireland, I found drawings from the Lord to visit Friends in England. I travelled through part of Wales and on to Bristol and London, and from thence to Surrey and Sussex ; then north to Cumberland and to Whitehaven, to take shipping. While waiting for the ship I had a great meeting there out of doors. From 1697 to 1713, I often travelled through Ireland and also in England.

" Within this space I was seven times at the Yearly Meeting in London, the Lord's good power accompanying me in His service.

" ' During one of these visits,' Samuel Neale tells us, ' at a great Meeting of Friends in London were two persons of high rank in the world, who sat very attentively while a Friend was speaking, and seemed to like what was delivered.

" ' When Thomas Wilson stood up, being old and bald, they despised him, and one said to the other: " Come, my Lord, let us go, for what can this old fool say ? " " Nay," said the other, " let us stay, *for this is Jeremiah the prophet*, let us hear him."

" ' As Thomas went on the life arose, and the power got into dominion, which tendered one of them in a remarkable manner : tears flowing in great plenty from his eyes, which he strove in vain to hide, and he stood up when the old man sat down, and desired he might be forgiven of him, and the Almighty, for despising the greatest of His instruments under heaven, or in His creation.' *

" Now, I having had it upon me from the Lord for a considerable time to visit Friends again in America, my dear ancient friend and companion, James Dickinson, signified to me by a letter, that he had a like concern to visit Friends again in those parts ; whereof I was truly glad, for we had often travelled together in great love, unity and sweetness.　So we agreed to meet in Dublin, and thence took shipping for America in the Tenth Month, 1713.　The name of the captain of the vessel was Richard Kelsey, of Whitehaven, in Cumberland.

" We took our voyage north about, and after

---

* Journal of Samuel Neale.

I had seen the captain's diligence, care and good conduct in his ship amongst his servants, and those on board, it drew my heart towards him in very much love, and gave me encouragement to have some religious discourse, wherein I found he aimed at justice and equity, so that my love increased towards him; and he being a man frequent in prayer, we entered into discourse on the substantial part of prayer. I told him: 'We could not pray at all times in words, knowing our own insufficiency, but waited for the assistance of the Holy Spirit to help us and guide our understanding; having regard to what the Apostle said: "I will pray with the Spirit, and with the understanding also,"—1 Cor. xiv, 15, which might be inwardly performed, although no words were outwardly spoken.' To which he readily assented, and told us: 'We might keep our meetings in the great cabin at any time when they did not keep theirs.' Now, though we had a storm in this passage for near a month together, yet the captain's prudent management of the ship, and shewing himself so very respectful to us, and the good conversation we had together, made our voyage much the pleasanter.

" On the Seventh day of the week, at night, the captain told us we should find the soundings next day, which we did accordingly about noon; then he told us, that if the gale stood, we should reach the cape that evening; so sailing on till near night, we were within about seven or eight fathom water; but night coming on, he wisely stood out to sea, and in a short time we got into Lynnhaven Bay, having been nine weeks in our passage from the sight of Ireland. We parted from our kind captain in great love. He would have us take some of his provision, and gave us much loving counsel, which we accepted kindly.

" We landed at Queen Anne's Town, and hired horses from thence to York River; next day we took boat to the western shore, from whence we contentedly took our travel on foot into the woods, having our saddles, saddle-bags, and great coats upon our shoulders. After a little time, seeing a man at a distance, riding towards us, James Dickinson said:

'Who knows but yonder man is coming to help us?' Who, when he came up, knew James, and cheerfully said: 'I had best alight and take your things upon my horse'; this we accepted of, and he went along with us to James Bates's house, who received us very kindly, his wife having been convinced by James Dickinson, and was a faithful Friend. It being their Weekly Meeting-day, we went along with them to the meeting, and had a good time.

"From Pennsylvania we crossed the Delaware River, and on our way a Baptist preacher came up to us, and, directing his speech to me, said he would ask me a question. I bid him say on. Then said he: 'My question is, What is the ordination and qualification of a true minister of Jesus Christ?'—To which I answered: 'The Apostle saith: "As every man hath received the gift, even so minister the same one to another, as good stewards of the manifold grace of God. If any man speak, let him speak as the oracles of God; if any man minister, let him do it as of the ability which God giveth: that God in all things may be glorified through Jesus Christ." '—1 Peter iv, 10—11. I further said mildly to him: 'Thou mayest see that the ability of a true minister is in the divine gift.'—Then he said: 'I have another question to ask, which is this: Can any man that hath this divine gift, positively deny the command of our Lord Jesus Christ?'—To which I replied: 'That no man that was faithful to his holy gift, durst deny the commands of our Lord Jesus Christ.'—'But,' said he, 'you do.'—I answered: 'Thou hast charged boldly, now thou must prove in what we deny them.' —He said: 'You deny water-baptism, which Jesus Christ commanded to be an ordinance in His Church to the end of the world.'—I told him he must prove his assertion, for I did not understand that ever Jesus Christ gave any commands to His ministers to baptize in elementary water; I desired him again to prove what he had asserted. Then he began to repeat many Scriptures, quoting chapter and verse. I patiently heard him, until he had gone on a great while; and I, seeing he had wrested the Scriptures, told him he must now make a full stop, till the company came up, for my companion had a Bible in his pocket; so standing still he came up, and the book was given to a young man, who was desired to read all the texts that had been urged to prove water-baptism to be a command of Christ, but finding no text to make good his charge, I opened unto him the true baptism of Jesus Christ, which is 'With the Holy Ghost and with fire.'—Matthew iii, 11. The Truth came over him. We parted friends, and he attended our meeting next day, and was silent.

" From Boston we went to Lynn, and thence to Salem, so to the eastern parts of New England,* as far as Dover, and returned by

---

* The circumstances related in the following extract from a Manuscript in the collection at Devonshire House, London, appear to have occurred in the course of this visit to New England :—

" In the year 1714, our worthy friends, Thomas Wilson and James Dickinson, came into this province on a religious visit to the churches. I was present at a meeting they had at Plymouth, which, on account of the great gathering of people, was held under the trees. Thomas, in the exercise of his gift in the ministry, was led to treat on several subjects, which, making great impression on my mind at that time, and tending to confirm me in the faith I made open profession of, I still remember. He spake largely on ' the captive maid ' in respect to her service to her lord and master, [2 Kings v, 2-4] and in a powerful manner set forth the privileges which the true members of the Church of Christ enjoyed under His way of Boston to the Yearly Meeting at Providence."

After extensive travel and service among Friends, Thos. Wilson and his companion turned toward the coast, in order to take shipping for England.

"Soon after we agreed with the master of a vessel for our passage, the ship being bound for Liverpool; but told him we had a desire to stay the First-day Meeting. He said, if he did not fire a gun, we might stay; and a little

---

peaceful government   He spoke prophetically concerning the work of sanctification some were under, saying, the Lord would bring the faithful through all, to His glory and the solid comfort of the afflicted, though some might be, like David, in the horrible pit, &c. This reached me in such a manner, that I was much broken, and said in my heart: ' Surely all here will be convinced, and not only convinced, but converted by the Eternal Word of God unto the true faith of Christ our Lord.' I thought none could withstand the doctrine preached, it being with great power and divine authority.

" The Friends at whose house they were to dine insisted on my going with them, and as this was on my way home, I complied. Being sat down in the house, Thomas Wilson fixed his eyes upon me, which made me conclude that he saw something wrong in me, upon which I arose and went out, being much affected, but heard him say: ' What young woman is that ? She is like the little captive maid I have been speaking of this day, the God of life strengthen her, she will meet sore trial, but if faithful, the Lord will fit her for His service.' These words have since been a blessing to me, when almost overwhelmed with trouble   Adoration and praise be to the Author of all our mercies for ever !''

before the meeting began, he fired a gun, which gave us warning to hasten aboard, although it was much contrary to our freedom, not being clear in our minds to leave the meeting; but we went on board. They set sail, but made little way that day, and we soon perceived that as the master of the ship had endeavoured to cross us, the Lord crossed him, for there arose a great storm that night, which continued several days, in which time the ship sprung a leak, which daunted them. Yet taking some courage again, they kept to sea; but the leak increased so fast that they altered their course and stood in again, and with some difficulty got to an anchor in Lynnhaven Bay; which brought a fresh engagement upon us of thankfulness to the Lord for so signal a preservation. Here the master concluded to unlade, that he might stop the leak, and told us we might go on shore and see our friends.

" We hired a boat and sailed up the river, so put to shore at the house of a widow woman, a Presbyterian, who received us kindly. She said she had heard of us, and that the New Testament made much for us. After we had eaten and drunk, we would have paid her, but she would take nothing from us, and when she had shewed us a little on our way, we parted with her in a friendly manner. That night we got to a Friend's house, and afterwards amongst Friends in Virginia. My companion, James Dickinson, and one Robert Jordan took boat, went aboard the ship and brought off our things ; the master then shewed himself very respectful, and said : ' If we thought fit to come again, we should be very welcome, and if not, we might use our freedom.'

" We went over the bay, and had a meeting with Friends at the same place where the captain would not suffer us to stay before. After this meeting we were free in our spirits to return, and in a little time after, we took shipping in another vessel, and landed at Cork, in Ireland, where we staid a meeting on the Sixth-day of the week. After meeting we went to Clogheen, and the next day to James Hutchinson's, where we lodged that night, and rode next morning to Mountmellick, where the Province Meeting for Leinster was then held. We went into the meeting, Friends being gathered before we came; and the power of Truth broke in upon the meeting, whereby Friends' hearts were greatly tendered under a sense of the Lord's mercy in preserving us; they not knowing anything of our being landed until we came thither.

" Here I parted with my dear friend and companion, James Dickinson, and as we had travelled together in great love and unity, we likewise parted in the same. He went to Dublin, in order to take shipping for Cumberland, and I returned home to my dear wife and family, being truly thankful that the Lord had brought us together again."

James Dickinson* on his part writes: " I parted with my dear companion, Thomas Wilson, in the love of God; we had travelled together, by sea and land, about 12,000 miles, *labouring to settle the people on Christ, the Rock and the Foundation.* The power of the Lord was wonderfully with him, and made him as a flame of fire against sin and wickedness; often, too, as a cloud full of rain, carried by the

---

* See Appendix B.

breath of the Almighty, to water the thirsty ground and comfort the afflicted.

" Before reaching Barbadoes we were chased by a man-of-war, but our eye was to the Lord. The company concluded to fight, and made preparations for it, having their places ordered them where they should be ; but the captain, knowing it was a matter of conscience to us, was civil and bade us go to the doctor if we pleased ; at which the passengers were very angry, saying we deserved to be shot. We told them Christ's Kingdom was not of this world, and therefore His servants cannot fight, but as the captain was so kind as to give us liberty of choosing our places, we would be on the quarter-deck with him, which greatly confounded those who were so much against us, and gave us an opportunity to set the testimony of Truth over them. But the ship proved to be an English man-of-war.

" My dear friend had much service in this last visit to America, and was greatly comforted in seeing the fruit of his former labour, many walking in the light of the Lord Jesus Christ.

" What I have said is only to attribute all to the Lord's power, to whom be praise and glory for ever, Amen."

Again resuming Thomas Wilson's Journal, in 1721, he writes : " I found a concern upon my spirit to go for England, and took shipping in Dublin in company with John Barcroft.* After two days at sea the ship struck on the sand, and in the morning lay aground, so that we got out our horses and went ashore in Wales." We find, that after ten months' extensive travel through England, the faithful labourer returned home much worn in body, and with his life-work almost accomplished.

He continues : " I stayed about home, visiting meetings, that Winter till Third Month, 1724. I went to Half-year's Meeting in Dublin, where I was greatly comforted in the feeling of the Divine Life and power, which is the

---

* John Barcroft resided near Edenderry in Ireland. He was the first Friend who came to settle in that neighbourhood after the wars, and was very helpful at that time to encourage a few families to meet together for divine worship. He proved himself very serviceable in that meeting, and it afterwards became large When about 33 years of age, he was called to the ministry, and was a diligent and successful labourer for the good of souls, both in Ireland and England.

H

crown and glory of our meetings. I then returned home, and growing infirm of body, went little abroad to distant meetings. Now I rejoice that I have served the Lord in my day. I feel great peace from the Lord flowing into my soul, and am thankful that I have been made willing to serve Him. My dear wife, being a woman that truly fears God, hath freely given me up at the Lord's call, so I hope she will have a share in the reward, and peace whereof He has given me the earnest. Having deeply travailed both in soul and body for the promotion of Truth in a general way, I have often besought the Lord that He would effectually reach my own children in particular, and be pleased to make them faithful witnesses for Him in their generation."

Thomas Wilson being taken ill in Eleventh Month, 1724, continued weakly for some time, He uttered many weighty expressions, and from time to time was concerned in earnest prayer to the Lord for the young and rising generation. He was fully resigned to the will of God, yet desiring, if He had no further service for him, to be removed out of his pain, which was at times great. When in less suffering he often spoke of the things of God. At one time he said : " If Friends kept the ancient path, and observed the Lord's rules, they would be a blessed people " ; and again sweetly and prophetically spoke words to this effect : " That a great harvest day was coming over the nations, and that the Lord would fit many and send them into the harvest " ; and again : " The Lord's goodness fills my heart, and I have an assurance of my everlasting peace in His Kingdom, with my ancient Friends gone before, with whom I had sweet comfort in the work of the Gospel." At another time he said : " Although the Lord has made use of me in His service, my trust is only in the mercy of God in Christ Jesus." He often expressed his desire : " *That Friends might dwell in humility, and keep low ; for that to his sorrow he had seen many who grew high come to ruin, both themselves and posterity, and their places left desolate.*"

He was preserved sensible to the last, and passed away without sigh or groan, as if he had been going to sleep, on the 20th day of the

H 2

Third Month, 1725. His remains were buried the 22nd of the same, accompanied by a great number of Friends and others; when Friends had a good opportunity to bear testimony to that Divine Power, whereby he was raised up to be a faithful witness for the Truth in his generation.

We now turn to his wife's testimony concerning her husband, which is found among ten or twelve other documents of a like character. These coming from Meetings and individuals in England and America, bear witness to this good man's worth and acceptance as a minister of the Gospel.

" THE TESTIMONY

Of MARY WILSON *concerning her dear husband, deceased.*

" SINCE it hath pleased the Lord to remove my dear husband by death, it hath often been a concern upon my mind to give testimony concerning him, which is as followeth :—

" Having good cause often to remember the times of our being first acquainted, I well remember, when he was come up to the state of a man, how he was restless in his mind, and earnestly desired the knowledge of the true God ; in which time, he went from one place to another, among the Church of England people, to hear what their priests could tell him of the way of salvation : for then his soul was in great want of a Saviour ; and great was his hunger after the way of life and righteousness.

" In this condition the Lord was pleased, in His unspeakable love, to visit his soul with the springing in of His light and power, by which he was much broken into tenderness, and brought into great humiliation and fear: in which condition he came among the despised people called Quakers; and although it was then a time of great persecution, yet did he sit down with them in their meetings, in silence, until such time as it pleased the Lord of heaven and earth so to fill his heart with His powerful word, that he knew the burning thereof as a holy flame in his soul: then was his mouth first opened in public prayer and thanksgiving to the Lord; and afterwards to sound the Everlasting Gospel, which was glad tidings to many poor, benighted souls.

" And further, I think I may safely say concerning him, that when he was sensible that the Lord had revealed His Son in him, and that a necessity was laid upon him to preach the Gospel, he did not consult with flesh and blood, but gave up unto the heavenly vision; and was willing to spend the flower and prime of his days in the service of Truth, which he did in many years' travel; and laboured much in the work of the ministry in England, Ireland, and America, before he married.

" In the fortieth year of his age, we took each other in marriage in Cumberland; and soon after came into Ireland, and settled near Edenderry; he having had, for some time before, some remarkable sight of that place, which he at times would speak of: and we had reason to believe it was our place, for the Lord blessed us together, and we had great comfort in that it was our lot to settle among such honest, tender-hearted Friends, unto whom we were nearly united.

" After we were settled, he was often engaged to travel in Truth's service; and I may say, from a certain sense that rests upon my heart, that the more he gave up to the work he was called unto, the more we were blessed : and although it was pleasant to me to have the company of so good a husband, yet it was more solid satisfaction to me to give him up to answer what the Lord might require of him. And I may say to the praise of God that I was made a sharer with him, in feeling the sweetness of that heavenly love and life that his heart was often filled with, and which streamed forth to the comfort of many ; for he was as a cloud that the Lord often filled and caused to be emptied, to the refreshing of his heritage. My soul, with many more, hath great occasion to bow in deep thankfulness unto the Lord, for the many refreshing showers that we have been favoured with ; and to give Him the praise thereof, who is worthy for ever.

" He was a loving and kind husband, a tender father to his children ; one that was laborious in the creation, and provided plentifully for his family; open-hearted to his friends, and beloved in the neighbourhood by such as knew him. He looked with a pitiful eye towards the poor of all sorts, and did administer unto the wants of many. He was one that delighted in justice and hated wrong things; and although the Lord blessed him in many ways, yet was not his mind lifted up thereby, but he continued unto the end an humble-minded man.

" He was often sorely afflicted in body, yet frequently travelled to visit Friends in much outward pain. In his last journey in England, he endured much bodily weakness, which continued upon him to his end; for he went no more abroad, only to our own meeting and twice to the Half-year's Meeting in Dublin. It was often afflicting unto me to think of being left behind: but what shall I say? the Lord hath done it; He have given and taken away.

" So the Lord hath brought my mind into quietness and contentment with my condition, and with what He hath done; steadfastly believing that He hath removed my dear husband in His mercy and favour, and received his soul into His everlasting kingdom. I shall conclude this my testimony, with fervent desires in my heart unto the Lord God Almighty, that He may, for His work's sake, favour His Church and people with a plentiful spring of a living ministry, and touch the tongues of many of our youth with a live coal from His holy altar; that many may be willing to run His errand, and be serviceable in His hand, as were many of the generation which He hath removed from us.

" MARY WILSON."

CHAPTER IV.

MOUNT WILSON AND HORETOWN.

WE have followed the course of a devoted servant of the Lord, and have heard him say, when nearing the heavenly shore, that amid his abundant labours at home and abroad he had earnestly besought the Divine blessing for his own children. These memoirs now lead us in the line of Thomas Wilson's son, Benjamin, whose signature, in conjunction with his brother's, is appended to the following document respecting his father :—

" We give this short testimony concerning our dear father, whom the Lord has been pleased to remove by death. We have no small share in the loss of him, but have great reason, with thankful hearts, to bless the Lord on his account, Who made him so great a blessing to us ; and not to us only, but to many more that had a sensible knowledge of him, and of his diligent care and counsel for the good of souls. This, in the love of God, so prevailed in his heart, that he was made willing to spend and be spent in that work and service, a faithful labourer in God's vineyard, that truth and righteousness might increase on this earth ; not accounting any fading and transitory enjoyment too near or dear to part with for Christ. He much delighted to see the youth among Friends grow up in a living, sensible concern for the Truth ; and desired that elders might be good examples and patterns in the Church, being careful himself to be found of this description.

" We could say much more concerning him, but rather choose to be brief ; referring to other testimonies given with respect to his labours, travels and services for the Truth: and shall conclude with sincere desires that the Lord may so favour us, through His infinite goodness and divine assistance, that we may thereby be enabled to run that race that is set before us, so as to obtain the blessing while here, and the crown of eternal life that is laid up for the righteous.

" THOMAS WILSON.
" BENJAMIN WILSON.

" *Thornwell, the 1st of the
Third Month,* 1727."

There is no record of Thomas Wilson, junr., but we know that Benjamin Wilson married, in 1724, Dinah, daughter of Joshua Clibborn. The latter was a son of a Colonel John Clibborn, an officer in Cromwell's army, and a man of strong character and considerable local influence.

About the year 1658, when twenty-six years of age, he came with the Army of the Parliament into Ireland, and settled on a property in Moate, King's County. His descendants still inhabit Moate Castle, the family seat.

Colonel Clibborn had a great aversion to the people called Quakers, and finding that they had a meeting-house on his land, he determined to clear them off by burning this house. Provided with fire he went to the place, when, as he supposed, it was empty, but to his surprise he found a meeting going on, and Thomas Loe preaching. He threw away the fire, sat down behind the door, and became so powerfully affected that his purpose was immediately changed. On his return home, his wife asked if the Quaker Meeting-house was burned. "No," said he, "If you will come to meeting there next Sunday, and do not like it, I will go with you to church the following Sunday."

She accordingly went, and Thomas Loe again preached. Both joined the Friends, and Colonel Clibborn built a Meeting-house, which, with a burial ground, he bequeathed to the Society for ever.

He was of a generous, open-hearted disposition, beloved and esteemed in his neighbourhood, very hospitable, especially to strangers who came on errands of love preaching the Gospel of Peace.

His situation in the Civil Wars, during the struggle of James II, to retain his power, was very perilous, as his house was only a few miles from Athlone, where the Irish Army had established their garrison, and from whence issued parties to distress the country.

Meetings were kept up at great hazard. Succouring many, and endued with Christian love, John Clibborn held on his way in patience and courage. He was one night dragged by his hair from that home which had been long a refuge for the distressed, but which was now the spoil of the plunderer, and in flames.

His life was attempted three times by the bloodthirsty foes around him, and at last they laid his head on a block and raising the hatchet prepared to strike the fatal blow. He called for a brief respite, and then knelt down to pray, as did Stephen, that the sin might not be laid to their charge. Just then another party arrived, and asked: "Who have you got there?" and were answered: "Clibborn." "Clibborn!" they echoed, "a hair of his head shall not be touched."

Escaping with his bare life, almost naked,

he wrapped a blanket around him and presented himself before the Commander at Athlone.

The officer desired him to point out the men who had been guilty of this outrage, and they should be hanged before his hall-door. But he refused, saying he bore them no ill-will, and only desired that his neighbours and himself might be allowed to live unmolested.

John Clibborn lived to see tranquillity restored, and ended in peace his long life in 1705.

In connecting himself with the family of this good man, we may believe Benjamin Wilson came into possession of " a prudent wife, which is from the Lord."

They made their home at Mount Wilson, near Edenderry, one of three farms owned by his father and uncle, Mungo Bewley. At this date there had settled about Edenderry a number of English colonists who had become Friends.

An old resident was wont to tell that when a boy his father objected to his going to school on the Mid-week Meeting-day, lest the child should run across one of the fifteen Quaker conveyances which frequented the road !

To gather in so many of those who were sturdy Puritan soldiers and officers, the power of the life and ministry of Friends must have been considerable.

About this time William Penn's life was consecrated to God, through the instrumentality of Thomas Loe, to whom reference has just been made; Sir William Penn, Vice-Admiral of England, had sent his son to Cork, where he had heard Loe preach. and having continued to attend meeting in that City, he was cast into prison. In after life he became the founder of Pennsylvania, a State which prospered without military defence for sixty years, or as long as Friends continued to govern it.

Another instance of the power accompanying the preaching of plain and often uneducated men, is to be found in a statement of an officer of Cromwell, written after the Battle of Dunbar, as follows :—

" As I lay at the head of my troop, I observed at some distance a crowd of people, and one standing higher than the rest; upon which I sent one of my men to bring me word what the gathering meant. Seeing him ride up and

stay, without returning according to my order,
I sent a second, who remained in like manner,
and then I determined to go myself.   When I
came thither, I found it was James Naylor, *
preaching to the people, but with such a power
and reaching energy as I had not until then
been ever witness of.   I could not help staying
also, although I was afraid to stay, for I was
made a Quaker, being forced to *tremble* at the
sight I got of myself.   I was struck with more
terror than at the Battle of Dunbar, when we
had naught to expect but to fall a prey to the
swords of the enemy.   The people in that
gathering, in the clear and powerful opening
of their inward state, cried out against themselves and implored mercy.   I clearly saw the
cross to be taken up, so I durst not stay any
longer, but got off, carrying condemnation in
my own breast.   But ever since I have thought
myself obliged to acknowledge on the behalf
of the Quakers, as I have now done." †

We shall now be obliged to turn our attention
to other scenes.

---

* See Appendix D.   † James Gough's Journal.

About the time that Thomas Wilson first saw the light, in 1655, there was representing Great Yarmouth in Parliament a tried fellow-soldier and friend of Cromwell, Major-General William Goffe. His father was Stephen Goffe, or Goughe, graduate of Magdalen College, Oxford, and Rector of Stanmar, in Essex, of whom nothing is known before 1590. He is mentioned as a good disputant and logician, and a very severe Puritan. He had a large family, and lost his wife after the birth of his fifth son.

In Stanmar Church there is a bronze plate inscribed: " Here lyeth Deborah Goffe, the wife of Stephen Goffe, preacher of God's Word, who died 8th day of November, A.D. 1626, aged 39."

The Rector placed his third son, William, in business in London, but ere long the young man quitted the desk and joined the Army of the Parliament, as Quartermaster ; he rose to high command, and married the daughter of Colonel Whalley, Cromwell's first cousin.

The oldest son, Stephen Goffe, jun., D.D., an Oxford graduate, became, amid the chang-

I

ing religious opinions of that day, a Roman Catholic priest, and was chaplain to Henrietta Maria, wife of Charles I, in Paris. He was one of those who tried to free the King from his confinement in Hampton Court, but was seized and committed to prison, and afterwards found means to escape.

In Paris we find him as superior of a distinguished order, acting as a common father to the English exiles, both Catholic and Protestant, during the Commonwealth. By the Queen-mother's order he was appointed tutor to the son of Charles II, Duke of Monmouth. "Goffe died in the house of the Fathers of the Oratory, Paris, Christmas-day, 1681 ; he was," says Wood, "considered a learned man and well read in the Fathers." *

Stephen Goffe's second son, John, became D.D. and Rector of Hackington, near Canterbury. From this living he was ejected in 1643 for refusing to take the Covenant, and cast into the country prison ; how long he remained there is not known, but in 1652, through the

---

* Anthony Wood's *Athenæ Oxonienses*

influence of his brother William, he was given the living of Norton, Kent, and also became Vicar of St. Stephen's.

In the fluctuating course of events the peaceful Quaker family, whom we left at Mount Wilson, married into the family of William Goffe, Major-General in the Protector's Army of Ironsides.

The career of William Goffe is interesting as a picture of his times. He could preach as well as fight, for in 1648 we find him taking part in the three days of humiliation and prayer, self-imposed on the Puritan Army at Windsor Castle. Troubles were accumulating. The King was a restive prisoner at Carisbrooke; the Royalists were watching for their chance to retrieve disaster; the Presbyterians, with the City at their head, were half inclined to return to their allegiance; the Scotch Army was marching upon London; Parliament was divided against itself; everything looked black for the army and its leader.

" Then," says Adjutant-General Allen (" a most authentic, earnest man," in Carlyle's phrase), " the army resolved ' to go solemnly to search out our own iniquities, and humble our souls before the Lord in the sense of the same; which, we were persuaded, had provoked the Lord against us, to bring such sad perplexities upon us at that day' . . . And at this time did the then Major Goffe make use of that good Word, Proverbs, i, 23: 'Turn you at my reproof: behold, I will pour out my Spirit unto you, I will make known my words unto you.' Which, we having found out our sin, he urged as our duty from those words. And the Lord so accompanied by His Spirit that it had a kindly effect, like a word of His, upon most of our hearts that were then present, which begot in us a great shame and loathing of ourselves for our iniquities, and a justifying of the Lord as righteous in His proceedings against us." *

One of the aims of this little series of memoirs is to enforce, by means of an object lesson, the peace principles inculcated by the

---

* In 1649 we find the following record : " On the departure of Cromwell for Ireland, his friends assembled at Whitehall, and Colonel Goffe, among others, expounded the Scriptures excellently and pertinently to the purpose "

Gospel of Christ. But although the universal Christian Church is being led to recognize these more and more, we cannot refuse to acknowledge that servants of God are found among those who, not seeing that the dispositions which lead to war are wholly incompatible with the spirit of the Gospel, have believed they wielded the sword for Him. William Goffe was a striking example of this fact.

After the expulsion of the Long Parliament, in December, 1653, he aided Colonel White to turn out the recalcitrant remnant of the Barebones Parliament.* Sherton's State Papers describe this as follows :—

"After the Speaker had left the House, with many Members, twenty-seven stayed behind speaking to one another, and going to speak to the Lord in prayer. Then Colonel Goffe and Lieutenant-Colonel White came in and desired them there to come out. Some answered they were there by a call from the General, and would not move unless they had a command

---

* State Papers, page 263.

from him. The Colonel returned no answer, but went out and fetched two files of Musque-teers, and as good as forced them out—among whom I was an unworthy one."

At Dunbar, Goffe commanded the Protector's own regiment, and in 1655 (the date of Thomas Wilson's birth) we find him one of the ten Major-Generals, under whose absolute control Cromwell has parcelled out the whole country. His district is Surrey, Hants, and Berks. England, wearied of plots and disturbance, settled down peaceably under their control, for they were, as Carlyle says : " Carefully chosen, of real wisdom, valour, and veracity; men fearing God and hating covetousness." Their duties were as various as their powers were great; among these being the selection of " Godly ministers " for the various parishes—a task for which these soldier-preachers were perhaps more fit than most military rulers before or afterwards.

In 1657, with Whalley and Berry, Goffe seems to have favoured the offer of kingship to Oliver, which their fellow generals opposed. About this date he was nominated for the

House of Lords, and two years later his name appears, with sixty others, on the death warrant of Charles I.

He had followed Cromwell through his campaigns in Ireland, and had fought at the sieges of Drogheda and Wexford, and for his services received large grants of land in the County Wexford, among them the estate of Horetown, which his descendants still hold.

His last public appearance in England was on May 25th, 1659, when he vainly tried to rally his regiment in defence of Richard Cromwell, urging him to arms to maintain his cause.*

We next find him as a fugitive in America, where he afterwards figured in one of the most interesting incidents in the early history of New England—the deliverance of the frontier town of Hadley from the attack of a barbarous Indian tribe.

Alarmed at the threatening aspect of events, the inhabitants had, on September, 1675, assembled for prayer, and to humble them-

* See Appendix C

selves before God in a solemn fast. While thus engaged, the terrible war-whoop was heard, and all seemed at the mercy of the band of approaching savages, who had partly gained possession of the town before reaching the Church.

At this crisis, amid the bewilderment and terror of the Colonists, there suddenly appeared among them a man, tall, and erect of stature, calm and venerable in aspect, with long grey hair falling over his shoulders. Rallying the retreating townsmen, he issued brief and distinct orders in a commanding voice, and with cool and soldierly precision. The powerful influence which, in a moment of peril and difficulty, a master mind assumes over his less gifted fellows, was well exemplified on that occasion. The stranger's commands were implicitly obeyed by men who, until that instant, had never seen him.

The town of Hadley was saved, and the inhabitants preserved from massacre ; after the first moments spent in anxious enquiry and thanksgiving, the Deliverer was eagerly sought for. Where was he ? All had seen him an instant before, but he had disappeared, nor was he ever seen again. One or two among the people could have told who he was, but they prudently held their peace.

Unable to account for the sudden advent and disappearance of the stranger, the people of Hadley believed he was an Angel sent from God for their rescue.

The story, however, is a historical fact, and although, with the traditions of the Indian War of 1673, this belief has been handed down among the New Englanders, the history of William Goffe accounts for the Delivering Angel of Hadley. After the death of Cromwell, when the Restoration was evidently close at hand, Goffe, well knowing that England would no longer be a place of safety for him, left Westminster in May, 1660, and, accompanied by Edward Whalley, his father-in-law, whose name stands fourth in the death warrant of Charles I, embarked for Boston.

On their arrival, both were well received by Governor Endicott and the leading men of the Colony. But, as the news of the Proclamation of Charles the Second came out in the same ship with them, it was considered prudent that they should retire to the village of Cambridge, now a suburb of Boston. There, any persons insulting the Regicides, were bound over to keep the peace, while in England a reward was offered for their heads.

But the peaceful days for the refugees at Cambridge were soon to end. Late in November, the Act of Indemnity, from which, among others, the names of Goffe and Whalley were excluded, arrived in Boston. When the Council met, the majority were against taking action. At a consultation of private friends, however, it was decided that Goffe and Whalley should proceed to Newhaven, in Connecticut. They were treated with kindness on the journey, and on arrival took up their abode with Mr. Davenport a minister eminent in the early chronicles of the Colony, for piety, learning, and zeal.

In March, news arrived from England that ten of the Regicides had been executed under circumstances of revolting cruelty.

These tidings, which Goffe and Whalley received with somewhat of pious exultation, were accompanied with others relating more immediately to themselves. A Captain Bredan, having seen the refugees in Boston, reported the circumstance in London, and Governor Endicott received a royal mandate to arrest and send them to England. He did not dare openly to resist this order, but attempted to evade it on the ground of inability to put it into execution. Two young Englishmen, zealous Royalists, offered, however, to arrest them, and immediately proceeded to New-haven. Letters had preceded them, and on the next Sunday Davenport preached a sermon divided into no less than thirty-two heads, from Isaiah xvi : " Take counsel, execute judgment ; make thy shadow as the night in the midst of the noonday ; hide the outcasts ; bewray not him that wandereth ; let Mine outcasts dwell with thee ; . . . be thou a covert to them from the face of the spoiler." This discourse had the desired effect. When the pursuers arrived, they waited on Governor Leet of Newhaven. Leet replied that a conscientious scruple prevented him from backing their warrant, and he would not suffer them to act as magistrates in Newhaven, but would send out his own constables to seek for Goffe and Whalley.

We need scarcely say Leet's constables did not succeed in arresting "the outcasts," but their retreat having become unsafe, they sought refuge in a cave on the summit of West Hill, one of the headlands that form the harbour, where, supplied with provisions by a woodman, they lived for about a month. The Cave of the "Judges," as the Regicides were invariably called in America, has long been one of the show places in Newhaven.

The pursuers, after visiting the Dutch Colony of Manhattan, now New York, returned to Boston and made a formal complaint against Governor Leet.

Matters began to wear a serious aspect. The Council was divided: some advocating the surrender of the "Judges," lest Royal displeasure might injure the infant colony.

At this crisis, Goffe and Whalley marched down to the Governor and surrendered themselves. Leet seems to have been unprepared for this bold step, and kept them in concealment, provisioning them from his own table for twelve days. It was concluded that Leet should continue to temporize and the Regicides return to their retreat, giving their parole that they would again surrender when required, In the Summer of 1661, the Colony made peace with the Government by proclaiming Charles II, and the pursuit of the " Judges " slackened for a time. At the approach of Winter they went to the house of a man named Tomkins, in Milford, where they remained for two years, and, though never wandering further than the orchard, their residence was known to many.

Goffe was a man of education, and famous in the Parliamentary Army as a " Preacher, prayer maker, and presser for righteousness and freedom." He distinguished himself thus while at Milford on all suitable occasions, to the great delight of his hearers. Milford, however, was not to be their final resting-place. Matters between the Colonies and the Mother Country being still unsettled, a commission was sent to New England, and the astute statesman, Clarendon, when advising this course, used the remarkable words :

" The Colonies are already hardened into republics." The duty of the commissioners included the arrest and transmission to England of Goffe and Whalley. Warned by this intelligence they left Milford in October, 1664, for the more remote town of Hadley. Travelling by night, and concealed by day, they reached a retreat provided for them by the minister of Hadley, a Mr. Russell, who had two rooms, an upper and a lower one, adjoining his own house, where, in utter seclusion, Whalley and Goffe lived fourteen years until the death of the former in 1678. It is not certain whether Goffe visited Newhaven after the death of his father-in-law, but it is almost certain that he, too, died in Russell's house about two years after.

Goffe, from the period of his departure from England until the year of his death, kept a diary. Unfortunately this interesting manuscript was burned at Boston, during one of the riots preceding the revolutionary war, but there are a few scattered extracts in the pages of Hutchinson and other New England writers which afford us a glance at the inner life and

THOMAS CHRISTY WAKEFIELD, SENR.

sentiments of the Refugees. Goffe regularly corresponded with his wife in England under a feigned name. Part of a letter, and his wife's reply, are before the writer of this history. They display great amiability of private character, and minds supported under the affliction of a life-long separation by strong faith in a happy reunion hereafter. Whalley suffered in both mind and body by the sad circumstances of his lot, being for some years quite imbecile, requiring Goffe's constant care. The only events during the prolonged sojourn at Hadley was a visit from John Dixwell, another of the English Regicides, and the attack of the Indians followed by Goffe's remarkable appearance as the deliverer of the town.

It is known for a certainty that Russell, in whose house they lived, buried the bodies on his own premises, but it is surmised that, to prevent discovery, he procured Dixwell to remove the bodies to Newhaven, where Dixwell had settled, unmolested, under the name of James Davis. Undoubtedly, the last resting place of Goffe, Whalley, and

Dixwell is at Newhaven. On the tomb of the latter is the following inscription: "J. D., Esq., deceased, March 18th, in the 82nd year of his age, 1688-9." On the tomb of Whalley there are only the initials E. W., and a date which at first glance appears to be 1658, but on more careful scrutiny the 5 is discovered to be an inverted 7, meaning 1678, the correct date of his death. The inscription on Goffe's tombstone, is merely "M. G., 80." But there is a dash thus — beneath the letter M., signifying it is to be read inverted as W., the correct initial, and the 80, which would seem to imply his age, denotes the year of his death—1680. This enigmatical mode of inscription was adopted evidently by Dixwell to avoid detection and desecration; it answered the purpose in a former age and has attracted attention at a later period, proving the identity of the remains that lie beneath.*

After Major-General Goffe's flight to America, frequent and affectionate correspondence was maintained between him and

----

* *Chambers's Journal.*

his wife, who, with their son Richard, retired to their estates in Ireland. His son married, in 1681, Hannah, the daughter of J. Chamberlain, of Portmarle, Co. Wexford. Under the earnest ministry of Friends at that day, it seems the Goffe's early joined the body. The Chamberlains were most likely English settlers, and it was probably to this J. Chamberlain that Besse in his " Sufferings of the Quakers," refers: " 1676, Wexford.—By warrant against him in Ecclesiastical Court, Jonas Chamberlain was committed to prison for nine months by Humphery Good, priest."

In 1721, Richard Goffe's son, Jacob, married Mary Fade, of Dublin, whose father, Joseph Fade, after a distinguished military career, had joined Friends.*

From the old book above quoted, we append another entry: " 1661, Dublin.—James Fade

* Sir John Barnard, the uncle of Mary Fade, who was Member for London, twice Lord Mayor, and whose statue stands in the Exchange, had been a Friend, and never ceased to wear the plain garb, though his Quakerism probably gave way through association with the world.

K

and twenty others taken out of their Meeting-house by a guard of soldiers, and committed to Newgate, by order of Hubert Adrian, Mayor." Another entry: " 1671, James Fade, Dublin, having about £40 due to him by one Ezekiel Webb, was by Webb subpœned into Chancery, and, because he would not answer on oath, believing it forbidden by Christ, who said: ' Swear not at all,' he not only lost the £40, but £70 more to get clear of the debtor." *

Of this Jacob Goffe, there is little record; we trace him, however, taking part in public matters connected with the Society. His name with that of James Fade, &c., is appended to a document addressed to King George II in 1744, signifying the fidelity of Friends during a time of disturbance in the Kingdom.

His portrait, as seen by the writer in Horetown, represents him as a man of stately Puritan type; the canvas bears the mark of a

---

* George Fox, in a Court of Justice, once addressed his accusers thus: "You say, ' Kiss the Book,' the Book says, ' Kiss the Son,' and the Son says, ' Swear not at all.' "

pike thrust—a relic of the 1798 Rebellion, when a party who probably entered the house to murder his son thus took vengeance on the portrait of the father.

The son of Jacob Goffe and Mary Fade bore his father's name, and married Elizabeth, daughter of Benjamin Wilson, whom we left in his quiet home at Mount Wilson, King's County.

Elizabeth Goffe was a woman of strong character, with an unwavering faith in the God of her fathers. She doubtless occupied a position of influence in the home to which her husband took her in 1769, where, under the pious and watchful care of the father and mother, a numerous family filled the old Horetown House. The quiet of their country life was disturbed in 1798, by the terrible " Irish Rebellion," which broke out around them. Into its causes and results we cannot enter here, but it carried in its train misery, suffering and death, and left behind that legacy of civil war—the bitter heart-burnings of religious and political animosity. County Wexford became the chief seat of warfare.

There, the priests appeared among the rebels, and murders on a large scale were perpetrated under their sanction.

During this trying ordeal, the Friends stood firmly by their peace principles, convinced that " They who defend war must defend the dispositions that lead to war, and those dispositions are absolutely opposed to the Gospel."*

Thus they joined neither party, but became the Friends of all, and experienced wonderful preservation from fire and sword.

Doubtless spiritual force rises in proportion to meet the emergency which God in His providence permits to overtake His children. So we find Elizabeth Goffe's fine qualities of mind and soul stand out in clearer relief as the furnace of trial tested them with increasing severity; but the part that she and her family bore in the struggle was but similar to that which very many Friends endured in those trying times.

We shall now turn to a simple account of the

---

* Erasmus

experiences of the Horetown family, written by the youngest daughter, Dinah Wilson Goffe, who was requested towards the end of her life to commit to paper some of her early recollections.

CHAPTER V.

DIVINE PROTECTION.

DINAH W. GOFFE writes :—

" It has often occurred to me that I ought to leave some little memorial of the preservation extended by our Heavenly Father to my beloved parents and their family, as well as of the remarkable faith and patience with which they were favoured, under circumstances of a very peculiar and distressing character.

" It was about the middle of the Fifth Month, 1798, that the County of Wexford in Ireland, became a scene of open rebellion, headed by B —— H——, a Protestant gentleman, and two Roman Catholic priests, John Murphy and Philip Roche. Murphy was chief instigator to cruelty and murder; he pretended to catch the flying bullets of the royalist troops, but was at length killed by a cannon ball. Roche, though more humane, was finally hung. The aims of the insurgents were various; some were more cruelly disposed than others; all determined to liberate themselves by force of arms from the unequal yoke, as they believed it, of the British Government, and to become a free people; some to bring all Ireland to Catholicism, &c.

" About ten days before the Rebellion broke out, a Roman Catholic gentleman, who resided near, called on my father, and desired to speak to him in private. He then informed him that the country would, in the course of a few days be in a state of general insurrection. My father replied that he could not credit it, for that he had frequently heard such rumours. The gentleman assured him that he knew certainly it would be so, and that he had procured a vessel, now lying at Duncannon, to convey himself and family to Wales, and that, as a friend, he gladly offered accommodation to our household. My father thanked him for this act of friendship, but said that it felt to him a matter of great importance to remove from the position allotted him by Providence, yet that he would consider of it and consult his wife. After having endeavoured to seek best wisdom, my dear parents concluded that it was right for them to remain at home, placing their dependence and confidence in Him who alone can protect, and who has promised to preserve those that put their trust in Him.

" The estate and spacious mansion, called Horetown, occupied by my parents Jacob and Elizabeth Goffe and the family, were situated about ten miles from each of the towns of Wexford and New Ross. The rebels formed two camps at Carrickburn and Corbett Hill, one on each side of the house, at distances of two and five miles from it. This central position caused a constant demand on us for provisions, with which the insurgents were daily supplied, and they often said they spared the lives of the family for that purpose.

" A day or two after the commencement of the Rebellion, two carts were brought to our door, and the cellars emptied of all the salt provisions, beer, cider, &c., which were taken off to the camp. Fourteen beautiful horses were turned out of my father's stables, and mounted in the yard by two or more of the rebels on each. Some, which had not been trained, resisted by plunging; but their riders soon subdued them, running their pikes into them, and otherwise using great cruelty. Much of our cattle they also took, and orders were sent each week from the camp at Carrickburn, to have a cow and some sheep killed, which were sent for at stated terms.

" Soon after the general rising and arming of the people in the County of Wexford, we were roused one morning by the sound of cannon at a distance, and quickly heard that there had been an engagement at a place called ' The Three Rocks,' on the Mountains of Forth, near Wexford, between the yeomanry and the rebels. After a severe conflict the former were put to flight, with great loss of life; sixty or seventy were buried in one grave.

" Two of my cousins named Heatly, whose

THE OLD MOYALLON HOUSE, CO. DOWN.

mother had married out of our Society, were officers in that corps, and escaped to our house under the cover of the darkness of the night. On their arrival, they found that their father and mother, and seven or eight children, had been turned out of their comfortable home, and had also fled for refuge to my father's, where they were affectionately received. We had all retired to rest when these young officers arrived. The thankfulness of their parents, who had never expected to see them again, passes all description ; they were much affected and immediately returned thanks, on the bended knee, for the preservation of their children. For some days the two young men remained in the house, hiding from room to room, sometimes under the beds ; as there was a frequent search for arms and Orange-men by the rebels. Some of the chief of these, having information of their being with us, called, demanding them to surrender, and offering them the United Irishmen's oath. This however they resolutely refused, saying they had taken the oath of allegiance to their sovereign but a few days before, and would never perjure themselves. On this one of the rebels laid his hand on his sword, and in great irritation said, were it not for the respect they had for Mr. Goffe, and that they did not wish to spill blood in his hall, their lives should be the forfeit of their refusal. At length my cousins left our house by night, intending to make their way to Ross, and took shelter in the cottage of an old Roman Catholic nurse employed by the family; but by her they were betrayed, and handed over to the rebels, who took them prisoners to the camp. The lives of these interesting young men were, however, remarkably preserved, after they had endured much hardship in prison.

" Two Roman Catholic men-servants, belonging to our family, and lodging in the house, were compelled to join the rebels to save their lives ; and were armed with pikes—the first we had seen. On my dear mother's hearing of their having these weapons, she sent to let them know she could not allow anything of the kind to be brought into the house, so each night they left them outside the door. They behaved quietly and respectfully throughout, generally returning home at the close of the day.

"The rebels set fire to the houses of many Protestants; and in the morning after the general rising, a Roman Catholic family, seven in number, came from Enniscorthy, apparently in great distress, saying they had left the town on fire. They received shelter and hospitable entertainment from my dear parents, and remained with us the whole time. My mother often remarked, with reference to her large family, that provisions from day to day were so wonderfully granted, that they seemed, like the cruse of oil and the barrel of meal, never-failing.

" About twenty persons surrounded our dinner-table each day, beside those in the kitchen, four of whom were members of our Society, which my mother considered a great advantage at that awful period. She frequently said that ' hind's feet ' appeared to be given her, in being enabled with extraordinary ease to get through the numerous household duties that then devolved upon her. Thus the gracious promise was verified in her experience: ' As thy days so shall thy strength be.'

" A rebel once inquired of her: ' Madam, do you think we shall gain the day ? '   Feeling it to be a serious question, after a pause she replied : ' The Almighty only knows.'   He answered : ' You are right, madam ; have a good heart, not a hair of your head shall be hurt ; but when this business is over, the Quakers are all to be driven down into Connaught, where the land is worth about twopence an acre, and you will have to till that, and live on it as you can.'   My mother smiled and said : ' Give us a good portion, for we have a large family.'

" Hannah and Arabella (afterwards Fennell) with Dinah W. Goffe, aged about thirty, nineteen and fourteen, were the only daughters at home at this time.   The two former usually walked three miles on First-days to the Meeting-house at Forrest, accompanied by two of the women servants, though they frequently met with interruptions on the way.

" One day some of the people said, as they passed the Roman Catholic Chapel : ' How they dare us by going through the streets ! If they persist they shall be taken and dragged

JANE SAWDWITH WAKEFIELD, *née* GOFFE.

to the altar of the chapel, and suffer the penalty of their obstinacy.' But my sisters passed quietly on. On one of these occasions they remarked that a strange dog accompanied them : it followed them for some miles, and when they got safe home could not be induced to enter the house, but went away. This circumstance, though simple, seemed remarkable at the time. I fully believe that their minds were not resting on outward help, but on that Omnipotent arm which was mercifully underneath to sustain. They were enabled regularly to pursue their way, and to unite with the few Friends that were permitted to meet, remarking those opportunities as being peculiarly solemn. Our dear parents would gladly have joined them, but were unable from the infirmities of age to walk so far, and had no horses left to draw a carriage.

" The family were always assembled for the purpose of reading the Scriptures, after the fatigues of the day were over, and one evening a priest coming in, as he often did at other times, perhaps to see what we were doing, remarked on the quietude which prevailed.

My mother said it was usually the case when the hurry of household cares had ceased. He said he came with good news—that we were now all of one religion the world over. My mother then inquired what it was, as she believed there was only one true religion. He replied, that an edict from the Pope had arrived, and that it proclaimed a universal Roman Catholic religion, adding that it was high time for her to put up the cross. She asked what he meant by the cross. He said: 'Put up the outward sign on yourself and your children.' She answered: '*That* they should never do, but she was thankful in believing that her Heavenly Father was enabling her to bear the cross, and that she trusted He might be pleased to continue to do so to the end.' I was standing near him at the time, when he put his arms round me and said: 'My dear child, we shall have you all to ourselves'; and, placing his hand on my father's shoulder, he said: 'Mr. Goffe, you shall be one of our head senators.' This unhappy man, we afterwards heard, lost his life in attacking a Protestant gentleman, on

THOMAS CHRISTY WAKEFIELD JUNR.

whose kindness and hospitality he had thrown himself, when his own house was burnt down by the English troops. To us he was uniformly kind, and we thought his attention might, under Providence, have had some influence on the minds of the rebels.

" Many hundreds were daily on our lawn, and our business was to hand them food as they demanded it. Their fatigue and the heat of Summer being exhausting, large tubs of milk and water were placed at the hall and back doors, with great quantities of bread and cheese. The servants were frequently obliged to stay up all night to bake bread for them, and my mother and sisters often made their hands bleed in cutting the bread and cheese—if not cut up, they would carry off whole loaves and cheese at the end of their pikes. They took carving knives and others of a large size from the pantry to fasten on poles, thus converting them into destructive weapons ; on seeing which, my mother had the remainder carefully locked up after the meals. At times they gave us dreadful details of their own cruelty, and of the agonies of the sufferers, to the great distress of my sisters and myself.

One day after a battle they related many such acts, and said they had had good fun the day before with the fine young officers, by tickling them under the short ribs with their pikes, making them writhe and cry out bitterly. I was handing them food at the time, and could not refrain from bursting into tears, throwing down what I had in my hand, and running away into the house.

" We were greatly struck by observing that, however outrageously a party might come, there were generally some among them who were disposed to promote peace. Such would say: ' You ought not to treat them so—the poor ladies who have been up all night making bread for you with their own hands.' One morning a most violent party advanced, yelling and swearing hideously, like savages intent on rapine, so that we fully believed they had formed some wicked design ; but two young men, who looked sorrowful and alarmed on our behalf, though perfect strangers, came forward, requesting we might all withdraw and shut the door, as they could not but dread the consequences if the party were allowed to enter the house. The young men stationed themselves on the steps of the hall-door, drew their great cavalry swords, and, flourishing them, declared that no one should pass ; pleading for us in the most kind and energetic manner— 'Why would you injure Mr. Goffe and his family, who are doing all they can, feeding and providing for you?' After a long struggle the company relinquished their evil purpose. The young men were quite overcome with the exertion and heat : my father warmly thanked them, and gave them silk handkerchiefs to wipe their faces, inquiring their names—one of them was called Denis —— of Gorey. On that occasion, many wicked-looking women were outside, evidently waiting for plunder ; and, when disappointed, they made frightful faces, and shook their hands at us as we stood at the windows. One of them was heard to say when they withdrew : ' You are a set of chicken-hearted fellows !'

" A severe conflict took place at Enniscorthy, the garrison being forced to surrender, and

L

many hundreds, as we were told, left dead in the streets. Two days after it, our Quarterly Meeting for Leinster Province was, in usual course, held there, and was attended by David Sands from America, a valued minister, who was then travelling through Ireland with Abraham Jackson as his companion. As they passed through Enniscorthy, the latter had to alight and assist in removing the dead bodies, which still lay in the streets, from before the wheels of the carriage. The meeting, though small, was said to have been remarkably solemn, as it well might be. Many other Friends with ourselves were deprived of the means of attending, by the want of horses which the rebels had taken.

" A barn, about a mile and a half from us, belonging to a gentleman who lived at Sculla-bogue, was used as a prison, in which about 250 persons, chiefly Protestants, were confined —men, women and children, some being infants in their mothers' arms. There they remained from Sixth until Third-day, without receiving any food, except some sheaves of wheat occa-sionally thrown in, that the rebels might have

JOHN CONRAN.

the amusement of seeing them scramble for the grains. On the day of the battle of New Ross, sixty or more of them were brought out on the lawn and offered, one by one, life and liberty if they would change their religious profession, but they all refused. Some, after being half tortured to death, answered: 'No; give me more powder and ball first.'

"Two of the prisoners, named John and Samuel Jones, had attended our meeting, though not members, and their case was a particularly dreadful one. Samuel was kindly supported by his wife, whilst he was unmercifully tortured; one limb after another being broken, and each time the question repeated: 'Will you have the priest?' Which he steadily refused, looking calmly at his faithful wife, and saying: 'My dear, I am not hurt; I feel no pain.' His brother also bore his martyrdom with firmness, and was put to death by slow degrees in a similar way. The wife, with admirable fortitude, stood between them when they were shot, and held a hand of each. She then implored the murderers to take her life also; but they refused, saying: 'They would not dishonour the Virgin Mary by killing a woman.' I saw her afterwards in deep afflic- tion passing our gate, as she sat in a cart with the remains of her husband and brother. On the same day—viz., the 4th of Sixth Month —-the barn was set on fire, and all the other prisoners (said to be 184) were consumed. Some of the poor women put their infants out through the windows, hoping to save them ; but the ruffians took them up on their pikes and threw them back into the flames. I saw the smoke of the barn, and cannot now forget the strong and dreadful effluvium which was wafted from it to our lawn.

" In the engagement at New Ross the in- surgents were defeated. This was an awful scene of conflict and bloodshed, continuing with but little cessation for nearly twelve hours. It is stated that 2,000 persons were killed. The king's troops retreated twice, and the town was in the hands of the rebels, when a reinforcement was understood to have come up and put them to flight. Some asserted that no reinforcement arrived, and that the assailing multitude fled when there were none to pursue them. General Johnston, who commanded the Royalists, said that the success of that day was to be attributed to Providence and was not the work of man. Several Friends of New Ross had previously retired to Waterford; others, who remained, were remarkably preserved, though the town was set on fire in different quarters.

" Previously to the burning of the barn, a company came one day with two horses, saying they had orders to take my dear father and our cousin, J. Heatly, to the camp—the latter being the father of the two young officers before-mentioned. It was nearly noon when they came and seized these two victims; and my mother having gone to give some orders in the kitchen, I ran to call her, saying they were forcing my father on horseback. On this she came out, and pressing through the dense crowd on the lawn, asked them peremptorily: ' What are you doing with my husband ? ' On their saying they were going to take him to the camp, she said, in the same tone : ' You shall not take my husband, for he is in poor health, and if you put him in prison I think he could not live many weeks ; he will be here for you at any time you wish, as he cannot leave his house.' They were then silent, and quietly relinquished their design. My mother remarked: 'We have got what you call protections from the generals.' These were sent for, and read aloud to this effect : ' Let no one molest Mr. Goff or his family, they being hostages to the United Army. Signed in the camp of Carrickburn by two generals, Harvey and Roche.' These documents had been previously sent without any request made by the family. The party were then satisfied, as related to my father; all entreaty was, however, unavailing with respect to my cousin, J. Heatly, who was taken away on horseback, amid the shrieks and cries of his afflicted wife and children.

" We afterwards heard that they soon made him dismount and walk ten miles to Wexford They then put him on board a prison ship on the River Slaney, where he remained until the insurgents were totally defeated. He witnessed many of his acquaintances and fellow-sufferers —said to be to the number of ninety-seven in all—taken out of the same ship and put to death, with very cruel circumstances, on Wexford Bridge ; but he and a friend of his had a remarkable escape. The prisoners were called out by two and two, and when it came to his and his friend's turn, he made some excuses for delay. The rebels continued calling for them from the deck of the vessel, with their bayonets pointed down towards them, but they still delayed going. At this juncture, a rumour reached their guards that the English Army were marching into the town ; and this report throwing them into a state of terror, the lives of the two prisoners were saved. It proved, however, to be only a few yeomen, boldly preceded by an officer of the corps, which had been defeated in the engagement on the Mountains of Forth. The rebels took flight in all directions, and Wexford was left in possession of the English, to the great joy of the loyal inhabitants, who had suffered many privations and cruelties.

"John Heatly often related the circumstance afterwards, saying that Providence had in an extraordinary manner saved his life. He had been many years in the navy. His house, Rock View, was occupied for some time by the rebels, who left it a complete wreck; and persons in the neighbourhood said it was most amusing to see the country people parading about in the silk and satin trains, which they took when plundering my cousin's property.

" A party, who assumed the rank of officers in the Rebel Army, came to our house one day, and directed to have dinner prepared immediately. On my mother's requesting the servant to lay the tables in the hall, they indignantly asked : ' Is it there you are going to give us our dinner ? Shew us into the best parlour in the house.' But on my mother assuring them that she had seen noblemen sitting in that hall, they became calm and satisfied. They then asked for spirits and wine—saying they would have some; and when my mother told them that there were none in the house, they were greatly irritated —still saying they must have some. On being spoken to by my mother in the singular number, they desired her not to say thee and thou to them, as if she were speaking to a dog;

and on her again saying thou to one of them, he flourished his sword over her head, and said, haughtily: ' No more of your theeing and thouing to me.' They ate their dinner, however, and went off peaceably.

On one occasion (which Dinah Goffe does not mention) when the rebels seemed confident of success, two of the labourers came into the house, and sitting down, rudely addressed their mistress, desiring her to prepare some refreshment, as they had now changed places, and she was their servant. Laying her hand on the shoulder of one of them with physical and moral force, she commanded the men to return without delay to their respective employments, a command which they at once obeyed.

" We were now informed that orders had been given to take my dear father's life, and my mother was most particular in keeping us all close together around him, saying that if our lives should be permitted to be taken, we might be enabled to support and encourage each other, or else all go together ! One day, about noon, a large company appeared on the lawn carrying a black flag, which we well knew to be the signal for death.   My dear father advanced to meet them, as usual, with his open benevolent countenance, and my mother, turning to me, said, with her sweet, placid smile: 'Perhaps my stiff stays may prevent my dying easily.'   On which the Roman Catholic who had taken refuge with us said : 'Have faith in God, madam ; I hope they will not hurt *you*.' She quickly pushed forward and joined my dear father, who was surrounded by a large party.   He observed to them, he feared they might injure each other, as their muskets were prepared for firing, when one of them replied : ' Let those who are afraid keep out of the way.' My mother distinctly heard one of them say : ' Why don't you begin ? ' and each seemed looking to the other to commence the work of death.   Some of them presently muttered : ' We cannot.'   At this critical moment some women came in great agitation through the crowd, clinging to their husbands, and dragging them away.   Thus a higher Power evidently appeared to frustrate the intentions of the murderers, and my beloved father was again graciously delivered. One man said there was 'no use in taking Mr. Goffe's life,' but his two sons, if there, should soon be killed, and then the estate would be theirs.

"One morning a most outrageous party advanced towards the house, yelling and roaring like savages, evidently with some wicked design, but two young men who looked serious, again interposed in our behalf and would not allow them to enter. Thus were the words of David fulfilled : 'The wrath of man shall praise Thee; the remainder of wrath Thou wilt restrain.'

"A young man, who, with his mother, kept a neighbouring public-house, used at that time often to walk into our drawing-room, lay his sword on the table, and amuse me and my young cousin by giving us his finely-decorated hat to admire. One afternoon he tried to prevail on us to go with him to the camp, saying it was an interesting sight, such as we might never have an opportunity again to see. We were then sixteen and fourteen years of age, and on my saying I did not think my mother would permit us to go, he desired us not to tell her, and promised to bring us safely back. My mother, ever watchful, was at this moment crossing the hall, and seeing us together, she came forward and inquired what he was saying. When we told her, she asked him how he dared to request the children to go to such a place. She then reasoned with us on the impropriety of listening to such invitations, saying that if we had once gone, she should fully have expected never to see us again.

" Three or four hundred English troops, accompanied by Hompesch's German hussars, at length landed at Duncannon Fort; this was announced by the firing of cannon early in the morning. On my mother's entering my room, I expressed much pleasure at the intelligence, when she replied: ' My dear, we must rejoice with trembling; having much to dread from their being strangers, and we know not what may be permitted; we have only to place our trust and confidence in Him who hath hitherto preserved us!' This little army formed an encampment on my late uncle Cesar Sutton's lawn at Longgrague, about two miles from us. The next day whilst we were sitting at dinner,

MOYALLON MEETING-HOUSE, CO. DOWN.   BUILT 1725.

" Bequeathed for ever, in 1725, by Thomas Christy, for a Meeting-house and Grave-yard for the people call'd Quakers, to and for no other trust, use, or purpose; with a right for Friends to pass and re-pass in a right line, from his house and through his gates to the Meeting-house."

one of the servants said the rebel forces were coming from Wexford in thousands, intending to surround the English encampment. The royal troops, commanded by General Moore, having had previous information, were, however, on the alert, and met them on the road near our house. We counted twenty-four pieces of cannon belonging to the rebels which passed the entrance. A dreadful scene, partly in our view, was now enacted, and lasted for three hours; the firing was awful! Having closed the doors and windows in the lower part of the house as much as possible, we all retired to an upper room, and there remained in a state of fearful suspense. It was a terrible sight, and deeply affected us, the cannon balls falling thickly about the house. On one of my sisters raising the window to look out, a ball whizzed by her head; and this, with many others, we afterwards found. At length, seeing the poor deluded people running in all directions, we learned that they were routed.

" Two soon came to the house to have their wounds dressed, which my sister Arabella did as well as she could; one had a ball in the cap of his knee, and both bled profusely; they expressed much thankfulness, and hoped they might soon be able again to fight for their freedom. A fine young man coming, who had received a severe wound in his side and shoulder, my dear mother used means to relieve him, and dressed him comfortably in clean linen, while he frequently exclaimed: ' Do, ma'am try to stop the blood. I don't mind the pain, so that I may but fight for my liberty.' Observing him in danger from the great injury, she spoke to him in a very serious strain, and also recommended his going to the Wexford Infirmary. We heard afterwards that he died on the way, a few hours after he left us. This battle was at Goffe's Bridge, on the 20th of Sixth Month. Several hundreds of the insurgents were killed, but not many of the military.

" Soon after the firing had ceased, we observed two of the cavalry moving slowly and suspiciously up our avenue; on which my father went down to the hall door, and advanced with a smiling countenance and extended arms to meet them. One, who was a German, at once embracing him, saying, in broken English : 'You be Friend—no enemy, no enemy,' and gave him the kiss of peace, adding : 'We have Friends in Germany.' We got them eggs, milk, bread, &c., to refresh them, after the excessive fatigue and excitement which it was obvious they had suffered.

" The evening before this engagement, one of my sisters, passing through the servants' hall, observed the coachman leaning on his arm, apparently much distressed. When she requested to know the cause, he hesitated and said he could not tell her ; but on her entreating him, and adding that she should like to know the worst, he said that he had heard it planned at the camp, that, if they conquered the royalists, we were all to be murdered, and the generals were to take possession of our house. He then added, weeping : 'Oh, our plans are too wicked for the Lord to prosper them !' My sister remarked that we trusted in a Power stronger than man, and able to protect us in the midst of danger ; or to that effect.

" During the night following this battle, our house was surrounded by Hompesch's cavalry, who slept on the lawn wrapped up in their grey coats. The next morning twenty or thirty of the officers breakfasted with us, and said that we had had a marvellous escape on the previous day; the cannon having been placed on the bridge, and pointed against the house to batter it down ; even the match was lighted, when a gentleman, who knew my father, came forward, and told them the house was ' inhabited by a loyal Quaker and his family.' They had previously supposed it must be a rendezvous of rebels, and feared, from its commanding position, that they themselves might have been fired upon from it. Some of the officers, being refreshed by their meal, even shed tears when they reflected on the danger we had been in.

" My cousins Richard and Ann Goffe of Hopefield, near Horetown, had been observed by ' the United Men ' to persevere in walking to Forrest Meeting whilst the country was in a state of rebellion, and were apprised that, if they continued this practice, and refused to unite in the Roman Catholic forms of worship, they should be put to death, and their house burned.   This threat brought them under deep mental exercise, accompanied with fervent prayers that they might be enabled to come to a right decision ; and, collecting their large family together, in humble confidence that best direction might be mercifully afforded, after a season of solemn retirement, they laid the matter before their children.   On this memorable occasion, the noble and intrepid language of Fade Goffe, their eldest son, then about seventeen years of age, is worthy of being recorded.   ' Father,' said he, ' rejoice that we are found worthy to suffer.'   His parents were deeply affected, and their minds became so much strengthened, that next morning, rising before daybreak, they all pro-ceeded to the meeting, and were enabled to continue to attend Divine worship without molestation expressing thankfulness in thus being permitted to accomplish what they con-sidered their religious duty.   Thus Friends remained regular in their attendance, and on the very evening before the meeting day, when

M

so many were to be destroyed, and their houses to be burnt, the power of the insurgents was broken by a decisive battle on Vinegar Hill, and during meeting the next morning not a few of the misguided people actually sought an asylum of safety in the Meeting-house. Many flocked with their families to the homes of Friends. In one place a Popish priest borrowed a Friend's coat in order to save his life, and in another a Protestant minister did the same, but was soon after found in his hiding-place by the river, and murdered by his enemies.

" The wonderful protection experienced by the Society, brought to mind what had been foretold by some of their ministers years before, and the prediction ' That in a time of trial which was approaching, if Friends were faithful, many would be glad to shelter under the skirts of their garments ' was indeed literally fulfilled.

" David Sands and his companion attended the meeting at Forrest, and, returning to Horetown, were joyfully received ; my dear mother saying that his visit reminded her of the good Samaritan pouring oil into our wounded minds. The three families now occupying our house all assembled with him on this solemn occasion, and his communication was truly impressive and consoling, inducing tenderness in all present. He first alluded to the deep trials we had suffered; then to the infinite mercy which had brought the family through them; afterwards offered a solemn tribute of thanksgiving and praise to the great Preserver of men, whose power had been so remarkably displayed for our protection, when surrounded by danger on every hand. It was indeed a memorable visit, for which thankfulness prevailed to Him from whom all consolation is derived. The Roman Catholic family had never before heard these plain truths so declared, nor witnessed anything of the kind; but they all united in prayer on their knees, and the mother said: ' I never heard such a minister as that gentleman—he must be an angel from Heaven sent to you.'

" The Rebellion was now at an end; but, though peace and order were partially restored

M 2

to our afflicted country; yet the sad consequences still remained. Not only houses in ruins, burned and torn in pieces by both armies, were to be seen in all directions, but many of the rebels who were outlawed took up their abode in caverns in the Wood of Killoughran, and sallied forth by night, to commit depredations on such of the peaceable inhabitants as had returned to their dilapidated dwellings. Twice they visited us, and on these occasions our sufferings were greater than on any during the Rebellion. My father had been urged to accept the nightly services of a guard of yeomanry, but always positively refused.

" On the first night, having all retired to rest, we were aroused by a terrific knocking with muskets at the hall door. My dear father raised his chamber window, and requested them to wait a few minutes, and he would open the door ; but they continued knocking still louder, and swearing most awfully until he went down. On his opening the door, they seized him, and instantly rushed up to his room, breaking a mahogany desk and bookcase to pieces with their muskets, and demanding money. My father handed them twenty guineas, which was all he had in the house; but they persisted in asking for more, and swore, in a most profane manner, that if he did not give them more they would take his life. I slept with a little niece in a room inside his, and we were entreated by my sister Arabella not to rise, as we should be of no use. I endeavoured to comply with her request, and remain quiet, till I heard a dreadful scuffle, and my father's voice exclaiming: ' Don't murder me ' ! I could then no longer keep still, but opened the door, and saw one of the men, dressed in scarlet regimentals, with full uniform, epaulettes, &c., rushing towards my father with a drawn sword in his hand. My sister intercepted it by throwing her arms round my father's neck, when the point of the sword touched her side, but not so as to injure her. In the struggle the candle went out, and they called most violently for light. The horror which I felt at this awful moment can scarcely be expressed. My sister went down towards the kitchen, and found a man standing at the foot of the first flight of stairs ; she asked him to light the candle, when he said she might go down, and he would stand guard and not allow any one to pass. This he performed faithfully, and she returned in safety. I could not, after this, leave the party, but followed them through the house. The dreadful language they used, some of which was addressed to my sisters, impresses me with horror to this day. Money seemed the sole object of their visit that night, as they repeatedly said: 'Give me more money I tell you'; assuring my father that if he did not give them more, they would murder him. They even said from minute to minute, while they held a pistol to his forehead : ' Now you're just gone.' They then forced him to kneel down, repeating the same words and presenting the pistol. Seeing his situation, I threw my-self on my knees on the floor and clung with my arms round him ; when the ruffians pushed me away, saying : ' You'll be killed if you stop there.' But my father drew me towards him more closely, saying : ' She would rather be hurt if I am.' They snapped the pistol several times which, perhaps, was not charged, as it did not go off. When they found there was no more money they desisted, asking for watches, which were given them, and at length they went away, after eating and drinking all they could obtain, and charging my father to have more money for them the next time or, they declared, they would have his life. So saying, one of them, who appeared in a great rage, and had a cavalry sword in his hand, cut at the handrail of the hall stairs, the mark of which still remains.

" About a fortnight afterwards, before the family withdrew to rest, my father had a presentiment that the robbers might come again that night, and sat up later than usual. About midnight they arrived, knocking furiously as before, and fully prepared to plunder the house. They soon emptied the drawers and took all the wearing apparel they could get, that did not betray the costume of Friends, so that we were deprived of nearly all our clothes. On perceiving that they were taking all, my mother begged one shirt and one pair of stockings for my father, which they threw at her face in the rudest manner, using dreadful language. They behaved most violently, and spreading quilts and sheets on the floor, filled them with all sorts of clothing, they then called for victuals to eat and drink, desiring my sister to drink their health, putting the cup of small beer to her lips and bidding her 'wish long life and success to the "babes of the wood,"' as they called themselves. This she steadfastly refused. They then declared they would come again in two weeks, and take us all to live with them in the wood, 'and cut bread and butter for the babes.' Their behaviour was so insulting, and my dear parents were so fearful of these threats being realized, that they determined on sending us young females to my cousins, Goffe and Neville, who were then merchants in Ross; and there we remained for some weeks, until tranquillity was restored to the county.

"After the robbers had finished their repast, they threatened to take my father's life, behaving very outrageously, and saying they must take him to their main guard at a little distance and murder him there, as they did not like to do it in his own house. They then led him out, and we all attempted to follow; but they pushed my mother back, saying that she should not come—it would be too painful a sight for her to see her husband murdered, which they certainly would do. It was very dark, but my sister Arabella positively refused to leave her father, and they allowed her to accompany him. Whilst crossing the lawn, the root of a beech-tree, projecting above the path, caused him to stumble; he then sat down, and said: 'If they were determined to take his life, they might as well do it there.' My dear sister stood by in a state of awful suspense. They rudely asked him if he had anything to say, telling him his time was come. On hearing this he remained quite silent, and they, not understanding it, hurried him to speak; when he said: 'He prayed that the Almighty might be merciful to him, and be pleased to forgive him his trespasses and sins, and also to forgive *them*, as *he* did sincerely.' They said that was a good wish, and inquired if he had anything more to say? He requested them to be tender towards his wife and children ; on which they said : 'Good night, Mr. Goffe : we only wanted to rattle the " mocusses " out of you,'—meaning guineas.

" When they took my father forcibly out of the house, my mother, though much distressed, was favoured with her usual quietude and composure of mind, trusting in the Lord, who had been pleased to support her through many deep trials, and then forsook her not. So strong was her confidence, that she even called to the servant for some warm water, to prepare a little negus for my dear father against his return ; when I said : ' It is not likely we shall ever see him again alive, for they are going to murder him,' she replied, with firmness : ' I have faith to believe they will never be permitted to take his life.' In about a quarter of an hour my valued and tender parent returned, pale and exhausted ; and throwing himself on the sofa, said : ' This work will finish me ; I cannot hold out much longer ' ; which proved to be the case.

" Remarkable also was the protecting care vouchsafed to my uncle, Joshua Wilson (my mother's brother), whose residence at Mount Prospect, near Rathangan, King's County, was forcibly entered by a party of Rebels. One night, after the family had retired to rest, they were aroused by a tremendous volley of musketry, which at once shattered the hall door; and a loud cry was raised of 'Arms, money, or life!' with most awful swearing. My uncle went hastily down in his dressing-gown, followed by his wife, who heard them exclaim: 'You are a dead man'; and seeing one of the men present a pistol at my uncle's head, she rushed between him and the ruffian, exclaiming: 'Thou shalt not, and darest not, take my husband's life, or touch him; for the arm of the Almighty is stronger than thou art.' The man appeared confounded, and let the pistol drop from his powerless hand; it was very remarkable that the whole party left the house soon after, without doing any further injury. This great shock, and the alarming state of the country at that time, affected my uncle so much, that he left next day his com- fortable and handsome residence, in which he had resided happily for forty years, and sailed for England, where he and his wife spent the remainder of their lives, at Taplow Hill, near London.*

"Many were the heart-rending sufferings that some families endured, being turned out of their comfortable homes, and spending many nights in fields and ditches. Others who still remained in their houses were wonderfully favoured with faith and patience under these privations, conscientiously adhering to the law of their God, and thus experiencing, to their humbling admiration, the Name of the Lord to be 'a strong tower,' in which the righteous find safety. On taking a retrospect of this awful period, and of the strength of mind

---

* After they reached Taplow, George III heard that an Irish Quaker gentleman possessed full information of what was taking place as regards the rebellion, and called on Joshua Wilson. When the King found he was in constant communication with King's County and County Wexford, he came often to Taplow Hill; riding up to the house, he would tap with his whip at the window, enter without ceremony, and then sit down, while Joshua Wilson read the latest accounts. The King would then convey the information to those in authority, and direct them as to where to send reinforcements, &c

The Queen was also in the habit of calling on Joshua Wilson's wife, whose advice and help she sought in the illness of one of the young Princesses

evinced by my beloved parents, sisters, and others, my heart overflows with living praise and thanksgiving to the Father of mercies and God of all consolation.

" The repeated shocks and trials, which my honoured father endured during these fearful times, were too great for his strength of body; and on the 23rd of Twelfth Month, in the same year, 1798, surrounded by many of his family, he gently and peacefully breathed his last, being then in his sixty-third year. Our merciful Saviour sweetly sustained him in faith and confidence; the Almighty arm being underneath to comfort and support him whilst passing through the valley of the shadow of death. He never expressed a murmur; but, in humble Christian patience and acquiescence with the Divine will, often evinced his thankfulness for the mercies received. To one of my sisters, whom he observed weeping a short time before his death, he said: 'Don't shed a tear for me, my dear; but rather rejoice and be thankful that the Almighty has been pleased to permit me to die in peace, with my dear family around me; and not by the hands of wicked and unreasonable men.'   He took my hand affectionately, and said: ' My dear child: I must leave you all '; and, after a pause, added: ' Keep near to the Lord, and He will be a Father and a Friend to thee when I am no more.'

"Horetown now passed to my eldest brother, William Goff, and my beloved mother removed to Dublin.   She survived her affectionate husband nineteen years, and died in that city in the seventy-eighth year of her age, in perfect peace.   For several years she was in the station of an elder;   always endeavouring to rule her own house well, she was accounted worthy of double honour, and much beloved by her many descendants.   Sixty children, grandchildren and great-grandchildren were living at the period of her decease, in the year 1817.

" She was grand-daughter of Thomas Wilson, an account of whose religious labours is published with James Dickinson's.   Her last illness was short, being caused by a paralytic seizure.   On the morning before the seizure she entered the drawing-room with an expression of countenance remarkably solemn, and kneeling at my side, engaged in fervent vocal supplication for her numerous family, that the blessing of the Most High might rest on them, and that He might be pleased to continue with her to the end."

When near the close she is said to have requested to be raised on her knees in bed, to pour out her soul for her children and descendants to the fifth and sixth generations. She was perfectly conscious to the last, and sweetly resigned to her Divine Master's will.

" It is comforting to have a well-grounded hope that, through the mediation and redeeming love of our blessed Saviour, the spirits of both my beloved parents have entered into the mansions prepared for the faithful ; and that they are, through unmerited mercy, united to the just of all generations, ' Who have washed their robes and made them white in the blood of the Lamb ' : to whom be glory and honour for ever and ever !

" I am the only one now remaining of twenty-two children, and ever felt much attachment to my parents, whose pious and watchful care over their large family in our early years, lives in my heart as a sweet memorial. This feeling, I believe, was cherished by all their children, now, I humbly trust, through unmerited mercy and redeeming love, united to them in that happy state, where all trials and sorrows are at an end, and where all is joy unspeakable and full of glory.

"The foregoing has been written from memory, after a lapse of nearly fifty-nine years, the affecting events being still vivid in my recollection.

"A sum of money was raised by Government to compensate the sufferers in property, and a portion of it was offered to my father, Jacob Goffe, with others, in consideration of the great loss and damage he sustained ; but, as a Member of the Society of Friends, and not taking arms in defence of Government, he felt that he could not accept it.

" DINAH WILSON GOFFE.

"Penzance, Cornwall,
   Twelfth Month 23rd, 1856."

To the foregoing account, Dinah Goffe adds the Record made by the Yearly Meeting in Dublin, 1810, which runs as follows :—

MOYALLON HOUSE, CO. DOWN.

"The minds of many Friends having been deeply impressed with a thankful and humble sense of the many mercies, preservations, and deliverances, which our Society experienced, during the commotions which prevailed in this nation, in and about the year 1798; it was thought desirable that some memorial of them should be preserved—as well in commemoration of those remarkable preservations, as to transmit to posterity some account of the signal mercy of the Almighty, who is indeed a shield to those who put their trust in Him.

"It seems not unsuitable to observe, that for years previous to the breaking out of the Rebellion in 1798, many of the inhabitants of this nation suffered great depredations, by persons breaking into their houses at night and demanding and taking their arms. In the years 1795 and 1796, the sundry Quarterly Meetings were concerned to recommend to Friends who had guns in their houses, to destroy them, which was united with and confirmed by the National Half-year's Meeting for Ireland, held in Dublin, in 1796, as appears by the following minute, viz. :—

N

" ' National Meeting, Fourth Month, 1796.

" ' The subject of some in profession with us having guns in their houses, which might be made use of for the destruction of mankind, and other instruments of a like nature, having come weightily under the consideration of Friends in the three provinces; this Meeting, under a solid feeling, is of the judgment that all such should be destroyed, the more fully and clearly to support our peaceable and Christian testimony in these perilous times.'

" It appears that the labour of Friends, to carry into effect this recommendation of the National Meeting, was attended with a good degree of success; such Friends as had guns having very generally destroyed them. We have abundant cause to believe that this concern originated from the influence of best wisdom, and that it was a means of lessening (in some degree) the shedding of human blood, as those weapons would probably have fallen into the hands of violent men; and likewise, that it tended to preserve some of the members of our Society, who might, if they had

had guns in their houses, in an unguarded moment of surprise or attack, have used them so as to take the lives of some of their fellow-creatures.

" The Winter Half-year's Meeting was, in the year 1797, discontinued ; and, as matters of importance to the Society might arise, requiring immediate notice, a Committee was appointed to meet as occasions might require, to consider of and assist in such things of that nature as should occur in the intervals between the Yearly Meetings, relative to our religious Society.

" The said Committee reported to the Yearly Meeting in 1800 :—

" ' We have attended to the cases of those Friends who have suffered in the late commotions, and believe suitable assistance has been afforded to such ; and that there are not now likely to be any further cases transmitted to the Committee. The amount distributed to those who appeared to stand in need is £2,852 15s. 10d., and the balance remaining in the hands of the Treasurer being £994 15s. 10d., we have come to the judgment that it be

N 2

returned to the different Monthly Meetings, in proportion to the sums sent up by them.' "

The following extract from the Epistle of the Yearly Meeting in Dublin, 1801, to the Yearly Meeting in Philadelphia, exhibits the singular preservation then experienced :—

" Your Epistle given forth in 1799, addressed to Friends in Ireland, we received, which feelingly carried with it genuine marks of strong affection and near sympathy with us.

" It is cause of humble thankfulness that the dispensation was not of a very long continuance, though many Friends suffered very deeply in their property while the conflict continued. A considerable sum was raised, which, under the direction and management of a National Committee, was administered to the relief of the sufferers, in such proportion as, from accounts transmitted of their loss and circumstances, they appeared to require. When their wants were supplied, there was a redundancy, which was directed to be returned to the subscribers ; so that we do not at present stand in need of making any other use of your brotherly offer of assistance than to express a grateful sense thereof. It is cause of thankful acknowledgment to the God and Father of all our mercies, on the retrospect of that gloomy season, when in some places Friends did not know but that every day would be their last, seeing and hearing of so many of their neighbours being put to death, that no member of our Society fell a sacrifice but one young man.*

" May the mercy and loving kindness of a gracious God, thus signally manifested, be so deeply impressed on our hearts, that the complaint taken up formerly respecting a highly-favoured people be not applicable to us: ' He forsook God which made him, and lightly esteemed the Rock of His salvation.' But in grateful remembrance of the Lord's gracious

---

" * The case of this individual, taken in contrast with that of the other members of our religious Society in Ireland, affords a striking evidence of the truth of our Lord's declaration, that ' they who take the sword shall perish with the sword.' He came to an untimely end, through his own want of faith, and inconsistent conduct. Alarmed for his safety, he fled to a garrison town in the County of . Kildare, took up arms, and put on a military uniform. The place was, however, soon after attacked and taken by the insurgents. He was killed with many others; while the relations whom he had quitted were preserved unhurt, without any external defence.

dealings towards us, and of the preservation we experienced in those times of imminent peril, may we be concerned to walk in deep humility and circumspection before Him. ' Happy is that people that is in such a case ; yea, happy is that people whose God is the the Lord ! ' And may we walk in all respects consistently with our peaceable principles, that so the excellency thereof may be conspicuous in our conduct, and the standard of truth and righteousness exalted amongst the nations, whereby we may be enabled, from living experience, to adopt the language of the royal psalmist : ' O Israel, trust thou in the Lord : He is their help and their shield ! '

" Read and approved in our Yearly Meeting, held in Dublin, the 30th of the Fourth Month, 1800, and in and on behalf thereof signed,

" SAMUEL BEWLEY.

" Clerk to the Meeting this year."

CHAPTER VI.

MOYALLON.

IN tracing the descent of the family we have in view, our attention must now be directed to Jane Sandwith, the sixth daughter of Jacob and Elizabeth Goffe. She was married in 1794 to Thomas Christy Wakefield, of Moyallon, County Down, and while her parents in County Wexford were undergoing the said experiences of the Rebellion, she, in her northern home, was tenderly watching over her first-born son. Joseph Wakefield, her husband's father, was an Englishman, whose family can be traced back for many generations in Westmoreland. He had been sent to the North of Ireland to learn the linen business, of which that part of the country had been the seat since it was established by the Huguenots in the Sixteenth Century.* He had married, in 1766, Hannah, daughter of Thomas Christy, of Moyallon,

----

* See Appendix E

County Down. Moyallon is in the Parish of Tullylish, formerly part of the property of the powerful family of Maginnis, Lords of Iveagh. It was forfeited in consequence of the part taken by the head of this family in the Rebellion and Massacre of Protestants in 1641. Like many other districts in Ireland, it was the scene of some of those incidents, which for ferocity and inhuman cruelty are probably unparalleled in Christian history. A body of Protestant women were driven across Lough Kernan in this parish in Winter, when the ice gave way and the whole party perished.

" In 1685," says Lewis in his *Topographical Dictionary*, " the townland of Moyallon was granted to a colony of the Society of Friends in England, whose descendants still maintain the settlement, and have contributed greatly to the prosperity of the surrounding district."

Here a Meeting-house, since renovated, was built in 1723, and in 1710 a member of the Christy family appears to have introduced the bleaching of linen, a new industry in that part of the country.

Thomas Christy, son of Joseph Wakefield,

was born at Laurencetown House, in County Down, in the year 1772. His mother was removed by death when he was seven years old, which proved a great loss to her family of little children. When very young Thomas was sent to school in Westmoreland, and on his return to Ireland, having entered his fifteenth year, was apprenticed to Joseph Richardson of Stramore, near Moyallon, to learn his father's business. We now refer to a short sketch of his life, written by himself.

"In consequence of my kind grandfather, Thomas Christy, having left me a well-established and profitable business and considerable landed property, I wish to express my gratitude to him, and to my kind and affectionate master, Joseph Richardson. It was a privilege to have been placed with him, and I consider it a mark of my Heavenly Father's care. I believe it was there that I first felt the tendering of my spirit through the ministry of a woman Friend, about my eighteenth year. The visitation was at times renewed, but alas, the vanities and follies of the world led me captive for years, to my great loss and injury. My disposition led me to associate with the thoughtless, and join in their maxims and amusements, one of which was the practice of hunting. Although unguarded, I was always careful to return home at the end of the chase and, possibly from a degree of pride, to keep what is termed 'good company'—to mix only in respectable society.

"In justice to my master, I must say he always kept a watchful eye over me. He was in the practice of taking me to meetings at home regularly, and very often to the Monthly, Quarterly and Half-yearly Meetings, and when the latter ceased, to the Yearly Meetings. These were seasons of instruction; the advice and counsel given have left impressions extending to the present time. My master would, on my retiring to rest, say: 'Thomas, be prepared and ready to go with me to the Yearly Meeting in Dublin to-morrow morning at four o'clock.' It was short notice, but I must obey. There was no use in making objections. This strictness, with the regularity observed in his house, trained me in habits of punctuality, which, I believe, have had a good effect through life. When the term of my apprenticeship ended. then commenced a critical period ; the yoke being taken off, I was left without restraint. In the pride of my heart the first step was to lay aside my plain garb, and clothe the poor body with the dress of that day. If mercy had been withdrawn in this season of my forgetfulness, what would have been the consequence ? My latter end miserable, and my soul lost for ever.

" When looking back on these things, how can I render acceptable praise to the great God and Father of our Lord Jesus Christ, who was sent to save us from sin, to enlighten our hearts, and to call us to taste and see what good things are prepared for those who love Him ? Whilst penning these lines, everything within me is humbled and contrited in consideration of my Redeemer's love.

" On leaving my master's safe abode, I returned to my father's house, and entered into partnership with the Friend who had the principal management of the linen and bleaching business during my minority. As habits of application had been formed, I gave close attention to business, except on days that I entered on field sports—so captivating to those who follow them.

" I thus made myself liable to a breach of the rules of our Society ; and kind Friends were not wanting in tendering admonition and advice, but I was like a deaf adder, till the Holy Spirit brought conviction to my heart ; although some serious falls from my horse caused at times reason to take the place of thoughtlessness.

" At this period my father removed to Waterford, and I remained at Moyallon, the residence of my grandfather, who left it to me. This was about the twenty-second year of my age. Many thoughts now occupied my mind. One was to attend to an impression that a young Friend named Jane S. Goffe, with whom I had become acquainted, was designed for me as a companion through life. This I firmly believe was in the ordering of best wisdom.

" The subject having rested long on my mind the time seemed come for me to proceed.

I did so by first acquainting my friends, and then by taking a kind friend with me, as was the custom of the day, to inform her parents. As they approved of it, I was left at liberty to make known my affection to the object of my love. She received the communication in a suitable manner, yet with great fear and tenderness, expressing an apprehension that the matter was one of so much consequence that it required deep consideration.

" Having requested her to weigh the subject, I left, and after some time I returned and had a favourable answer. Words cannot sufficiently convey my thankfulness for such a blessing as was thus dispensed to me.

" It was the Lord's doing, and we were permitted to live in love and harmony for more than forty years. A better wife no man ever had ; her heart overflowed with love to me, to her children, and to all around.

" She abounded in kindness and generosity to the poor, her mind was stayed on her God, and through life she endeavoured to serve and obey Him as ability was given. Our children were tenderly brought up, and as they increased in years our thoughts were much engaged for their improvement in those things that would in future life add to their comfort and everlasting good." Here we may interrupt this true and tender eulogy by saying that her children did indeed rise up to call her "blessed." She was enshrined in their memory as a loving, wise, and Christian parent. One of her sons,* in his ministry of the Gospel, has often been heard to tell how the first prayers framed by his infant lips were dictated by his dear mother, and in early manhood, before he had entered the good Shepherd's fold, how her love and counsel followed him. " A gentle and familar step would be heard in the stillness of his chamber, and the mother would be at his bedside, a feeling having taken possession of her mind that her son needed a word in private, or that he might be wishing to join the hunt on the morrow."

And as the speaker described how timely and touching such counsels proved in his experience, and how the proud spirit of youth

---

* C. F Wakefield.

bowed under the power of his mother's love, deep feeling has spread over the audience while he has pleaded with mothers respecting their privilege and power in leading their children early to God.

To return, after our digression, to T. C. Wakefield's account: "Soon after our marriage," he says, "we were, in the year 1796, on a visit to Friends in Mountmellick, attending the Quarterly Meeting, and taking tea at a Friend's house. Thomas Scattergood, from America, was present. After a time of silence he addressed me in such a powerful manner that I was broken to pieces, and through adorable mercy was favoured to see the way of salvation opened before me. I earnestly prayed that my steps henceforth might be so directed that His peace might be my portion, and that heavenly wisdom might keep me from becoming a prey of the grand adversary of my soul."

Under the Divine power accompanying this address at this Friend's fireside, it would seem that the young man, through faith, entered there and then into his inheritance among the family of God.   An eminent writer,* says truly : " There is no condition for receiving salvation, but an empty hand to receive Christ."

This blessed experience became a preparation for what was so soon to happen.   About a year later a subtle heresy began to manifest itself among Friends in the North of Ireland. . The life of early Quakerism which led to devotion of body, soul and spirit to God had been declining.   Prosperity and ease took the place of the active and aggressive Christianity so conspicuous in the founders of the Society.

An effort was made by multiplying rules and restrictions to provide a substitute for that vitality which comes alone through the entire surrender to God, following on a recognition of the claims of Christ.

The delusion above mentioned, very similar in some respects to a certain phase of our " Modern Thought," took form through the preaching of a minister from America.   It was presented under the guise of extreme

---

* Archbishop Usher.

spirituality. During this time of decline, as the study of the Holy Scriptures was neglected, they were not used as a test to discover and condemn the false teaching.

Through exalting the inward at the expense of the written Revelation, the soil was prepared for this form of unbelief. It spread rapidly until most of the prominent members of the body were infected by it. A division took place and the affairs of the Church were left in the hands of a small number of younger men, who held their ground, through divine strength, well and wisely.

In the North of Ireland there was not a minister of the Gospel left, except John Conran, who had entered the body by convincement.

Among the few young men on whom the burden rested, T. C. Wakefield bore his share. He became Clerk to the Meeting, and in time occupied the office of " elder," while his wife performed her part, loving and being beloved as a mother in Israel.

We again return to T. C. Wakefield's journal : " Not long after my marriage a spirit of

o

delusion laid hold of those who were as pillars in our Church. They mistook imagination for revelation, and placing their dependence thereon, were led from step to step into darkness, until that divine light was obscured which would have preserved them from doubting the authenticity of the Holy Scriptures, and the divinity of our Lord and Saviour Jesus Christ.*

" To the young and inexperienced this was an awful time. They beheld men and women,

---

* It is well known that the founders of the Society of Friends based their doctrine and practice, as they believed, on the testimony of the Bible, according it the honour due to a divine revelation. Robert Barclay gives it as " a positive maxim that whatever any do, pretending to the Spirit, which is contrary to the Scriptures be accounted and reckoned a delusion of the devil."

Isaac Pennington says : " That light which comes from the same Spirit which the Scriptures come from, cannot teach things contrary to Scripture."

" By one offering He (Jesus Christ) hath perfected for ever them that are sanctified ; and we are not redeemed with corruptible things, but with the blood of Jesus Christ, as of a Lamb without spot ; and we have an Advocate with the Father, Jesus Christ the righteous, and He is the reconciliation for our sins, and not for our sins only, but for the sins of the whole world He is our righteousness, and sanctification, and redemption ; God hath made Him so, and we are justified freely by His grace, through the redemption that is in Christ Jesus, and therefore by the works of the law there is no flesh justified. That we are justified by faith in Christ Jesus, which works by love, is not denied by the Apostle, nor us " — EDWARD BOURN, *in reply to a pamphlet against Friends by Dr. Good,* 1675.

who had been objects of divine love, fall, and carry with them those who were weak in the faith. How can I sufficiently magnify the Shepherd of Israel, that in the riches of His mercy to me and my beloved partner, we did not also become a prey to the enemy? When nothing to the outward sense was to be seen but many falling on the right hand, and many more on the left; in adorable mercy the wing

---

On the divinity and sacrifice of Christ, George Fox, on being asked by Stevens why Christ cried out upon the Cross: " My God, my God, why hast Thou forsaken me?" made answer: "At that time the sins of all mankind were upon Him, and their iniquities and transgressions with which he was wounded, which He was to bear, and be an offering for them as He was man, but died not as He was God. And so, in that He died for all men and tasted death for every man, He was an offering for the sins of the whole world."—G Fox's Journal, 1st edition, page 4. And again:

" We own and believe in Jesus Christ   in whom we have redemption through His blood, even the forgiveness of sins . . . we own and believe He was made a sacrifice for sin, who knew no sin; that He was crucified for us in the flesh without the Gates of Jerusalem; and that He was buried, and rose again the third day by the power of His Father for our justification.

" This Jesus, who was the foundation of the holy prophets and Apostles, is our foundation. . . . He tasted death for every man, shed His blood for all, and is the propitiation for our sins. . . . 'Behold the Lamb of God, Who taketh away the sin of the world.' . . . . He saves from sin as well as from hell and the wrath to come. He has now come in the Spirit, and given us an understanding that we may know Him that is true."—*Extract from George Fox to Governor of Barbadoes.*

O 2

of divine love overshadowed us during the storm."

In the words of one of their own writers, we may add : " The Separatists did not disassociate as a body, or form a new sect, nor have they joined themselves to any *other* society. The considerations and circumstances which led to their separation have been various. Under the influence of these, they have acted as *individuals*, independent of each other, and responsible solely each for his own conduct and opinions."

It was remarkable that the individuals and families who embraced what in America was called the Hicksite doctrine, either left the country or seemed to melt away, so that in the course of years many homes stood empty and desolate.

About this date occurred the Rebellion of 1798, of which we have before made mention, and, although the North of Ireland did not suffer from its effects in their worst form, yet the Yearly Meeting exercised much care that Friends should be preserved from a warlike spirit, and that all fire-arms should be destroyed. Thomas C. Wakefield was then a young man of about twenty-five. and in after years he used to tell what a very great cross it was to him to obey this mandate, especially in the case of a new and valuable gun. However, in company with other members of the Meeting, bent on a similar errand, he wended his way to the River Bann, and, standing on the old " White Bridge" and breaking his gun, he consigned his portion of the sacrifice to the deepest depths of the stream.

Whether the like prompt obedience could be reckoned on at the present day is uncertain, but it became a means of blessing and preservation in 1798. The experience of Friends at that time reminds us of events that happened in the United States at an earlier period.*

---

* The reader of early American history may remember a deadly warfare carried on by the Indian tribes against the European settlers. The Indians lay in wait in highways and fields, and shot those who came within their reach without warning ; also attacking the settlers in their homes, scalping some, and dashing out the brains of others.

From this horrible warfare the Europeans sought shelter by leaving their homes and retiring to fortified places ; those who could not do so provided arms for their defence. Amid that time of desolation and terror the Society of Friends, who formed a considerable proportion of the population, were steadfast to their

Immediately after the decisive battle of Vinegar Hill, Thomas C. Wakefield took his wife to see her dear father, who had suffered much physically under the trials of the previous few months.

As their carriage entered Enniscorthy, they found barricades blocking their way, and the channels stained with human blood.

After leaving the town their coachman came to a halt, crying out: " We are all lost, a rebel crowd is bearing down upon us." Thomas C. Wakefield got up to look out, but his wife immediately put him aside, saying: " Hide thyself, and let me deal with the men." As they approached, she leaned out of the carriage window, and speaking pleasantly, said: " I am on my way to Horetown to see my father,

---

principles. They would neither retire to garrisons nor provide themselves with arms. While their neighbours were flying to forts they continued to pursue their ordinary occupations abroad and at home without a weapon for annoyance or defence. And what was their experience? They lived in security and quiet. The habitation which, to his armed neighbour, was the scene of murder or the scalping knife, was to the unarmed Quaker a place of safety and peace. Three of the Society were, however, killed; two of these, who, in a moment of weakness, obtained weapons to defend themselves, were shot dead by the Indians, the third was killed while flying to a fort for safety.

Jacob Goffe; can you give me any tidings about him? I am anxious to hear." At once remembering the kindness received from her father, they became friendly, and replied: "Mr. Goffe is alive and well," and saluting, they rode off, wishing her a happy meeting.

Again, referring to Thomas C. Wakefield's journal, he says: "I continued for many years in my outward occupations, which were prosperous; but believing there was a right time to cease from labour, in the year 1828 I gave up my business, apprehending that it was my dear Master's will. I am satisfied it was so, as peace followed, and I was set at liberty to attend to things more substantial than adding house to house.

"My talent is indeed small, but such as it is I try to use it to His praise, who alone is worthy—worthy to be honoured and obeyed."

In the year 1836 the great sorrow of his life overtook him, and though he lived to number nearly 90 years it was never forgotten. In Cheltenham the devoted and tenderly-loved wife and mother was called very suddenly to her heavenly home.

In writing to one of his children, the bereaved father says: "Every day since thy dear mother came to Cheltenham, her unbounded love for all mankind shone ever more conspicuously. Every object had a claim on her bounty and consideration, for she felt more satisfaction in spending her money on others than applying it to her own use. So remarkable was the expression of her countenance for some time past, that the last evening she was in our carriage the occupants of another, which passed us, remarked to me afterwards that it was ' heavenly.' How little did I think it was our last earthly journey ! I do most sincerely believe she was prepared to enter the heavenly rest, and that her purified spirit is now united with saints and angels in celebrating the praise and glory of the Lord God and the Lamb immaculate.

" Let us, who are left behind, try to treasure up her counsels, so faithfully and often given, and endeavour to follow the dear, dear departed, as she followed her Lord and Master, Jesus Christ. Of this I am well persuaded— she had no greater joy than to behold her beloved children walk in the Truth.

" The dear remains were deposited in the new graveyard in Gloucester—a beautiful spot."

Here, many years afterwards, he was himself laid beside the beloved wife of his youth, to await the resurrection morn.

The latter part of his life was spent in Torquay ; for he had left the old home in Moyallon to his son, C. F. Wakefield. The last entry in his diary runs thus : " Fourth Month, 1860.—The effort becomes greater as age advances to record the many mercies and blessings poured down on one who is compassed with infirmity. I am at times made mercifully sensible of the love of a gracious Father marked conspicuously in many ways— none greater than in bestowing on me an affectionate family. My beloved and dutiful daughter watches over me night and day, and ministers to both mind and body."

After an illness of seven months, he peacefully closed his long life on the 18th of Sixth Month, 1861.

CHAPTER VII.

THOMAS C. WAKEFIELD.

ONCE more we advance another generation, and follow briefly the life of the eldest son of the family.

Thomas C. Wakefield was born in 1796, and, as we have intimated elsewhere, in troubled times.

Religiously and politically a dark cloud hung over Ireland. The Roman Catholic Rebellion was fermenting, and in the Society of Friends a great heresy was imminent.

Nurtured in the vivid memories of these sad experiences, a lasting impression was made on the mind of Thomas C. Wakefield.

He held through life with unwavering firmness to peace principles, to a devout appreciation of the Holy Scriptures, and the importance of giving the great work of re-demption through the sacrifice of Christ its due place in Christian teaching.

His love and reverence for his mother lasted while memory held her seat. How often have his children heard of her beautiful face and noble presence, and of little incidents which marked her character in its benevolence, hospitality and kindness to the poor; how his mother would seek out the small shops on which to bestow her custom, especially wishing to encourage young people who were making a start in business.

Among all those who shared her house and home, none were so welcome as ministers of the Gospel, and he would tell how much " Mother " valued and anxiously expected through such, a message from their Master in " a family visit "; and when the children, probably well content to have escaped the religious address, would say: " Mother, the Friend had ' no opportunity ' with us," she would sadly reply: " Ah, my dears, I fear we are unworthy to receive such favours ! "

When very young, Thomas C. Wakefield was sent, under the care of a man servant, to school, near London, with a younger brother. Their first voyage from Dublin to Holyhead occupied a week. Under these circumstances of tedious travel by sea and land, the intervals were long between the holidays spent at home. Both mother and son were very fond of flowers, and in returning from school this was not forgotten, and even at the present day there blooms a cherished Polyanthus, which "I brought home for mother."

Having finished his education in England, he returned at the age of eighteen to settle at home, endowed with refined taste, mental culture, and engaging manners, which, had they been sanctified early by Divine grace, would have well fitted him for a life of usefulness in the Church, and in the world. At this critical period the Holy Spirit met him with a soul-tendering visitation, and under His blessed influence he sought lonely places to read and weep and pray. He saw the cross prepared for him to bear after Jesus. But the covenants made in those hallowed moments gave way in the day of trial, and this golden opportunity, the most precious crisis in life's history, passed away.

Soon after this, in 1817, he married Marianne Wilcox, and with every worldly prospect gay with promise he removed with his young wife to reside near Dublin. Here, amid the fascinations of society and the enjoyment of field sports, the still small voice was well-nigh silenced. Yet the Father's eye still followed the wandering child, and again a message of love was sent to bring him into the service of the King. But as the tender morning call had been disregarded, this time it came with a voice more stern and imperative. A fever that baffled medical skill arrested his course of pleasure, and brought him to the border of the grave ; indeed, so nigh, that the three physicians in attendance believed him to be dead. During these weeks of illness there had been much sorrow in his childhood's home. There, received as an honoured in-mate, lived the old minister who had alone stood his ground when the tempest of infidelity had swept over the little Church. Bowed before a prayer-hearing God, John Conran*

* John Conran was at times remarkably led by the Holy Spirit On one occasion a young man, while walking to Moyallon Meeting, said to a companion : "I wonder if that old fool will preach us a

pleaded for the son of the family whose kindness had sheltered his old age ; as he pleaded, an answer of peace came, and a message was sent on this wise to the devoted mother: " This sickness is not unto death, but for the glory of God."

One morning, while that mother was standing over what was pronounced to be the bed of death, a relative, the third doctor in attendance, addressing her, said: " Aunt Wakefield, what has now become of old Conran's prophecy ? " And yet it was to be according to the old man's faith, for, as the physician spoke, a faint sign of life passed over the pallid features, and the invalid was raised up to regard this illness in its true light. Deeply humbled before the Lord, he renewed his covenants, broke away from his gay associates, and returned to the neighbourhood of his old home to begin life anew.

Again the enemy was at work, suiting his

sermon to-day ! " After the meeting was gathered John Conran arose, and before proceeding with his address, said : " It may be that some one here has in his heart or by his lips asked the question : ' Will the old fool preach to-day ? ' "

temptations to the young man's state of mind, his suggestions being accompanied with just that element of truth which is sufficient to render his reasoning so seductive : " He had stumbled and fallen, he was too weak and too unworthy—would bring only dishonour on the cause he loved."   And so, under the guise of a false humility, the cross was again rejected, and again he refused the distinct call to the ministry of the Gospel. Thus, as he was wont to say in after years, was the honour and happiness forfeited, which his Lord held in His hand of blessing to bestow, and the crown placed on the head of his " younger brother."

Thomas C. Wakefield now lived a simple country life, and became much interested and very useful in the concerns of the Society. His house was one of old-fashioned hospitality, where the poor were, if possible, more welcome than the rich.

In many respects his mind was in advance of the times in which he lived. He came boldly forward to help the Temperance move-ment in its very early struggles, when unpopular among Friends, and despised in the eyes of the world.

Not long after the " Seven Men of Preston " bound themselves to Temperance reform, there was quite a sensation in the school-house at Moyallon, when, on the occasion of the first Temperance address ever given in the district, " the master " rose in presence of his workmen and proceeded to sign the Temperance pledge. When they had followed his example, the next proceeding was to clear the wine from the cellar and begin a Temperance society. His children remember how the Temperance lecturers were then welcomed to their home, whether it might be the veteran John Hawkins, from Birmingham, or Whitfield, the Newry blacksmith. The good work thus took hold, while his friends shook their heads, thinking, as " pledges were only for drunkards," that " Mr. Wakefield was demented."

His daughter has often told that, when very young, she was taken by him to see Father Mathew administering pledges in the street of a neighbouring town. With a great desire to become possessed of a shining medal, and her father's permission granted, the child made the promise amid the kneeling peasants, and although the medal was soon lost, the pledge has been honoured through life.

In the library of the Old Moyallon House, principally conducted by the dear mother of the family, perhaps the very commencement of First-day school work among Friends in Ireland, was inaugurated and carried on.

Liberal and enlightened, the parents were ready to unite on a common basis with all Christians in fellowship and good works* Avoiding political agitation, Thomas Wakefield's influence was on the side of religious

---

* An interesting occurrence may here be mentioned. His wife's family were Episcopalians, and whilst enjoying Christian fellowship with them, he maintained the spirituality of the Gospel dispensation. It is believed that his influence, and that of his wife, was felt among them. His brother-in-law, a clergyman in Norfolk, visited his father on his death-bed, and before leaving, requested the privilege of together partaking of the Sacrament, but, to the young man's surprise, he replied : " My dear son, I have the substance, I do not need the shadow." Disappointed and distressed, the young clergyman returned to his charge, and a few months after lay down himself to die. His mother now proposed that the same service should take place as had been so much desired in his father's case. " Ah ! " said he, " I could not at the time understand my dear father's refusal, but now I, too, am feeding on Christ, and I need no outward sign."

P

toleration. He had a happy manner of drawing Roman Catholics into conversation and friendly feeling, often affirming that there was but one true religion, the work of God in the heart, producing love to all men, to which they would often cordially assent. On the 12th of July, the anniversary of the victory won by William of Orange over the Roman Catholics, when in the old garden the " blue " columbine and " orange " lily, among other summer flowers, were in their glory, the children were not allowed to "shew their colours," by wearing the badges, as did others, for " the feelings of their Roman Catholic neighbours must be respected and considered."

But all through life, by his refusal to obey that early call, he felt God was saying to him : " *Yet one thing thou lackest.*" This fact was the means, he believed, of clouding his spiritual experience, and filling his cup of life with many deep sorrows. These pressed so heavily on his sensitive nature, at one period, as almost to make shipwreck of his faith.

After more than threescore years of his

pilgrimage had passed, a great affliction overtook him, through the sudden death of his dear wife and a beloved son, both absent from his side when they were called away. This was another waymark in life's history. His heart and home now desolate, in mental and spiritual anguish he cast himself in total surrender on Him Whose tender mercy faileth not. After this period his voice was occasionally heard in our Meetings, and he held with acceptance the station of Elder, though he would sorrowfully say: " Ah ! 'tis of little use now ; alas, my early unfaithfulness !" But He whose mercy is great unto the heavens had in reserve a sweet eventide for the weary traveller. A simple, childlike repose in the love of Him who spared not His own Son, took the place of unavailing regrets for the past, and the lack of assurance of faith for the future. After a Winter's residence abroad, he was gently and safely guided to his daughter's home to die, and there the promise was abundantly fulfilled : " At eventide it shall be light." Very sweet during that declining day was the atmosphere of his sick room, very touching his patience and deep humility, while the mercy of God through Christ Jesus filled his lips with praise.

A few extracts taken from notes during his illness will end the memoir.

14th of Eleventh Month, 1878.—Lying very low and prostrate, the dear invalid said : " ' Though I walk through the valley of the shadow of death, I will fear no evil.' I want to lie at the feet of Jesus ; I want to enter into Christ's sufferings ; but none of us can understand those words : ' My God, my God, why has Thou forsaken me ?' "

15th of Eleventh Month.—He exclaimed : " Precious Saviour, let me lie at the foot of the Cross and look up there. Thou art my only hope. Oh that forgiving love and mercy ! The peace I have had at times has been unspeakably sweet " ; and again, " Great has been my poverty of spirit." It was said to him : " My peace I give unto you." He responded : " What a peace ! and how remarkable the goodness that has brought me home, a poor, unprofitable, sinful creature ; but it is mercy, mercy, mercy ! Oh that precious blood ! "

On the 17th he remarked : " It can't be long

now ; it will be a glorious change. Since this illness I have often contemplated death, never with any fear, sometimes with rapture. There was a time when I feared death ; that was in the days of disobedience to God's will. How sweet it will be to meet on the other side ; it will not be very long, and I hope you will be all there."

On the 18th, after seeing two relatives, he said : " I love them, but I wanted to say the gold of this world bears a different stamp to the gold of the heavenly kingdom. How poor are all the treasures of earth ; I have nearly done with them all."

On being told a sick Friend was very dull, fearing his faith was not genuine, our dear father quickly responded : " Ah, he may expect these plunges. I know the experience ; brightness will come out of it, but there is no way out but by keeping the eye imploringly fixed on Christ."

19th of Eleventh Month.—After prayer to-day he joined solemnly in the " Amen." Lying very low, scarcely able to articulate, he lifted up his hands, and with raised eyes exclaimed :

" How good the Lord is ! " When his grandson entered the room he brightened up and said : " My dear boy, watch, watch against the Enemy. Keep the eye on Christ, my blessed, blessed, Saviour ; what would I do without Him ? "

On his son-in-law coming in to take leave for a day or two, he thus addressed him : " The Lord bless thee and keep thee. He will bless thee for thy works' sake, although works can never save us."

In an interview with his brother he said : " It is very sweet to have such unity of spirit, to feel thee so very near ; but we shall be nearer still, and shall sing praises and join in that glorious anthem. I love you all ; I love every one. If we enter heaven, it must be on the wings of love."

To his grandchildren, to whom he was tenderly attached, he said : " You must all be banner-bearers, and valiant too ; I don't think there will be one missing " ; and, smiling sweetly, added : " You don't know how much I love you. Is this not like Jacob blessing his children ? "

On the 22nd, fearing her dear father was quite unconscious, his daughter got up beside him on the bed, saying : " Bless the Lord, O my soul, and forget not all His benefits." He immediately raised his eyes and lifted his hands, while praise seemed to shine in his dying face. He made the same response when the words were repeated : " He was wounded for our transgressions; He was bruised for our iniquities." This was his last act of consciousness, as he fell asleep " looking unto Jesus," 22nd of Eleventh Month, 1878, aged 83.

CHAPTER VIII.

JOHN G. RICHARDSON.

THE second daughter of Thomas C. Wakefield, Jane Marion, was born in the year 1831, in the old Moyallon House (since consumed by fire), the residence of her great grandfather, Thomas Christy. From this house the family moved to England for the education of the children, but, after three years, were obliged to return to a property and residence in County Kildare, impoverished by the non-payment of rents consequent on the Irish famine. Here in Ballytore Meeting, Jane Marion Wakefield was married, in 1853, to John Grubb Richardson, whose memoir closes this book.

" From childhood I was strongly impressed with the duty we owe to God in caring for the welfare of the people around us."

Perhaps few have more faithfully and persistently carried out in life such an aspiration of childhood, expressed above in his own words, than the subject of this brief memoir, which is written with the desire to exalt His grace, Who, by working in willing hearts to will and to do of His good pleasure, develops and carries to a blessed fruition those aspirations which He implants, sometimes in very early life.

In a few rough notes, found after his death, John Grubb Richardson briefly reviews his earlier life, but it is a matter for regret that the sketch does not extend to later years. He says : " I have been frequently asked to write a little sketch of my life, and have become willing to give a few facts. I was born in Lisburn, County Antrim, in the year, 1813, where my father lived and carried on the linen business. My grandfather left his early home to learn the business from an uncle named Hogg, and our family has thus been connected with this industry for about 150 years.

" My excellent father and mother were of the generation of the righteous. They had ten children, seven sons and three daughters —a very united family. We were members of the Society of Friends, our forefathers having been convinced of Quaker principles by the preaching of William Edmundson in 1660. All our ancestors came from the north of England in Cromwell's army, and received grants of land from him to settle in Ireland. My father's mother was a lovely character. She was descended from Captain Nicholson, who, when quartered at Alnwick, married Lady Betty Percy, and was killed in one of Cromwell's smaller battles in the north of Ireland. A touching story is told of the young wife, who wandered over the battle-field, looking for her husband, with her babe in her arms. The circumstance was reported to Cromwell, who gave the widow a grant of land, which the family still holds.

" My maternal grandmother, Sarah Grubb, was known in the Society of Friends as the Queen of the South.' She was a noble and vigorous woman, loved and esteemed by a large circle, and, as a widow, managed her late husband's affairs and those of her orphan nephews and nieces—the family of her deceased brother, a banker in Dublin. She died at eighty, leaving a large property."

It is very characteristic of the writer to

mention the women rather than the men of his family; for with him it was a favourite saying: "Women do far more good in the world than men!" and again, in advocating the cause of Temperance in public and private, he would often say: "Gain the women and the doctors, and the cause is won!" But to proceed :—

"I was sent at the age of eleven to the once celebrated school in Ballitore, County Wicklow, kept by the Shackletons for three generations, where Edmund Burke was educated."

He often told his children how he early rose to good standing among the lads, by the result of a forced combat, instituted to prove the rank to be accorded to the new-comer, when he vanquished a much stronger boy by the use of his left fist—an art learned from an old servant at home. He continues :—

"At the age of fourteen, I was sent to Frenchay, Gloucestershire, to the leading school of the Society of Friends in that day. I left this school in 1830, at the age of seventeen, and went home to take my place in my father's business—contrary to my personal wish, for I had a great desire to become a barrister."

" It may be profitable here to allude to two
incidents in my early life, which, under the
direction of the Holy Spirit, were the means
of shaping my future course, by causing me
to reflect on eternal things.

" My father's coachman was proud of his
master's sons—there were seven of us—and
was very desirous to teach us to ride and drive
well ; he encouraged us to hunt, a favourite
amusement of my eldest brother, who was a
capital horseman. My dear, good father was
much opposed to our doing so, partly on
account of the waste of time, but more
especially because he dreaded our association
with those who led a life devoted to sport
and amusement. I had no means of hunting
except by taking one of my father's carriage
horses, as my eldest brother only was furnished
with a riding horse. After a considerable
struggle in my mind, by advice of the old
coachman, I yielded to the temptation. We
had a good run, but, on coming to a narrow
lane with a stone wall on each side, instead of
taking one wall at a time, as the other trained
horses did, my horse, a good jumper, made a

spring for both, and with the effort shot me over his head on the far side. There, having fallen on my head, I lay unconscious for perhaps an hour, one of my friends brought my horse back, fearing that I had been seriously hurt or killed. I slowly made my way home, reflecting on my position. What would have been the result, I meditated, if I had died there, having taken my father's horse to do that of which he disapproved ? I was brought to a firm resolution to seek forgiveness, and also clearly to see that if I, the second son of a large family, should devote my mind to field sports and other amusements, I would set a bad example to my brothers and be of little use in helping forward my father's interests. I never hunted again, but devoted my time to building up the family business.

" The second incident occurred about a year after the foregoing, and when I was twenty years old. Leaving the west of England in haste to reach home on account of the dangerous illness of one of my brothers, I landed at Cork, and, though it was Winter, I travelled night and day on the outside of a mail coach. I caught cold and was brought near to death by inflammation of the lungs. The doctor asked my father's leave to tell me that, if the mercury that I was taking, as a final resource, did not check the disease, in a few hours I should be dead. He did so in as gentle a manner as he could; but oh! how unfit I felt to die, and appear before a just and holy God, knowing that in many things which men might call small, I had been disobedient to the Holy Spirit's teaching. I did most earnestly entreat my Heavenly Father to raise me up again, and made solemn vows to live a more devoted life."

We may interrupt the narrative here by saying that in later life, about the year 1880, inflammation of the lungs again overtook him very suddenly. He rang his night-bell, and, on the appearance of a faithful servant, he said: "I believe the last message has come, but it is sweet to rest in the arms of my Saviour." He was, however, spared for a little further service.

To resume the personal record: "During

these early years I was powerfully visited by the Holy Spirit, and longed to be a more devoted and decided Christian. The ministry of Joseph J. Gurney, Elizabeth Fry, and Stephen Grellet, deepened these impressions. I remember carrying about Bunyan's ' Pilgrim's Progress,' and going into quiet corners to read and weep over the struggles of Christian. I should like to say here that I had great religious support from a beloved sister who had been a Christian from childhood. Indeed, through life I have been greatly blessed by the influence of women ; God in His great mercy gave me two very superior wives, who were as angels from Heaven to me. Surely I cannot say too much for feminine influence, and my earnest prayer is that it shall be more and more recognized at home and in public. Indeed, when I think of all the good influences surrounding me from childhood, I only wonder how little fruit I have brought forth in my life.

" From 1838 to 1841 I was much occupied with settling my younger brothers in business. It was my great desire that the seven brothers should be bound together and help one another through life.

"After starting a mercantile house in Belfast, we established another in Liverpool, and in 1841 I crossed in one of the first steamers to the United States, and assisted in establishing my brother Thomas as agent there.

" All these operations so engaged my mind that I lost much of my religious strength ; and business, alas ! so absorbed my thoughts that it measurably drove out spiritual things ; yet I loved the cause of Christ, and desired at some time to become a true and devoted Christian.

" In 1844 I married Helena Grubb, of Cahir Abbey, County Tipperary, a distant cousin of my own. Though brought up in a gay family, and loved and admired by the fashionable circle which surrounded her, she had chosen the better part when 14 years of age ; and, after some acquaintance, she accepted my offer of marriage, being impressed by the Holy Spirit that I was to be her companion for life. A more beautiful character never lived. . . .

" In extending our business, in partnership

with my brothers, we were obliged to keep pace with the times and become flax spinners and manufacturers. We had then to decide where we should build linen mills. I had a great aversion to be responsible for a factory population in a large town like Belfast; so, on looking round, we fixed upon a place near Newry, where had been built the first mill for spinning yarns in Ireland. With water power, a large population around, and in a country district where flax was cultivated in considerable quantities, it had moreover the desirable condition in my sight of enabling us to control our people and do them good in every sense—*and from childhood I was strongly impressed with the duty we owe to God in looking after the welfare of those around us.*

" In 1846 we began to build at Bessbrook, and the next year work began there. I had long resolved that we should have a Temperance population in our colony, though not until afterwards a total abstainer myself. The place came largely under my care and supervision, though I lived in Belfast, except in the Summer months."

Q

Here we may introduce some reminiscences written by his eldest son :

" My earliest recollection of my father must have been when about three and a half years of age, for it was previous to the death of my mother. It consists of his wrapping me in a shawl and carrying me in his arms from the house to a large shed where an entertainment was being given to the Bessbrook workpeople. This must have been in 1849, so that the latter were not so numerous as at present ; nor were his wishes on Temperance matters as clearly understood among them as they soon afterwards became, for I have a very certain, though confused, recollection of his pleasure being marred by finding out that the ubiquitous whisky bottle had been ungraciously and ungratefully introduced upon the sly.

" From this time forward, during some years I was his very constant companion when he was at home, and especially when on horseback, on which occasions it was his delight to take me out with him on a pony of wonderful speed and spirit, and yet little larger than a large Newfoundland dog.

" Several of his letters written to me about this time, when away from home, are still treasured, and a quotation from one of them may not be out of place, as shewing the bent of his mind even then :

" '*Fourth Month* 24*th*, 1850.

" ' MY DEAR LITTLE SON,

" ' I hope is a good little boy, and that the wooden horse I bought for him is not hurt. A nice little boy about his own age has made him a present of a little ship to sail on Bessbrook pond.

" ' I was very happy to hear that he did not beat Eliza (the nurse), but put down his hand before he hit her. This was the Bad Spirit chased away by the Good Spirit. Papa hopes he will always (?) be able to do so.'

" Such was the *first* letter received from an honoured father, and in strange harmony with its spirit—though conveyed in language suited to the experience gained by its recipient during the intervening space of almost forty years—was the last letter of importance received from him shortly before he was taken from us in 1890, which concludes as follows :

" ' I feel the weakness of age creeping over me, and want to see thee in thy *very* right place :

Q 2

Yet sure there is a warfare,
  No eye but Thine can see;
Oh hear my cry for succour,
  Come Thou and fight for me.
This self I cannot conquer,
  This will that still is mine;
Oh take them both, Lord Jesus,
  And make them one with Thine.

" ' May the Lord bless thee, guide thee, and teach thee, every step of the way, prays thy loving father.'

" The lessons inculcated in these days of childhood, when he and I were so much together, were easily learnt, and, needless to say, will never be quite forgotten.

" One was a consideration for the feelings of servants.

" Another was that mere leisured idleness was an evil thing, and that even little boys enjoy their pleasures more when they feel they have earned them. Thus I can never remember receiving pocket-money, in the way of being given to me by my father, until I went to school; but he was always ready to pay me well, if I was inclined to earn it.

" Picking and rooting up dandelions and other weeds was a large source of income, also the trapping of rats and mice, which in those days of wheat-growing were very numerous in every farmstead.

" But side by side with this idea of earning, my father was ever anxious to implant another, which was that even a child's earnings are rendered doubly sweet by being shared with others—especially with the poor.

" From his conversation in those days, I became early impressed with the idea of looking to the character of a person rather than his position, and remember my father often telling me how he would never take off his hat when, as a youth, he happened to see George IV or William IV in some public procession, not feeling any respect for their private characters, but that when by any chance he saw a well-known figure in those days in the London streets—the Iron Duke of Wellington—his hat went off, as he used to say, ' in spite of himself.'

" It was probably this tendency to look closely to the private characters of our prominent statesmen which prevented him (though taking a most keen interest in politics) from being a strong party man, or a ' thick-and-thin ' supporter of either great party in the state.

" His sympathy, however, in the main ran with the Liberal party until 1886, and to that party he was often able to give valuable support; indeed, I do not hesitate to say that he was the means of turning more than one local contest in their favour.

" His confidence in Mr. Gladstone seemed to decline from the hour he deserted the late William Edward Forster, and he often grieved that, when master of the great majority which placed him in power in 1880, Mr. Gladstone was so supine on the subject of Temperance. It is scarcely necessary for me to say that he regarded the Home Rule policy as pregnant with evil, both for Ireland and the Empire. He was a great admirer of the Earl of Derby, father of the present Earl, and who, as Lord Stanley, passed the National Education Act for Ireland, when Chief Secretary. He also was a warm admirer of Sir Robert Peel, both as a statesman and a man of the highest and purest private character, but in his later days, like many others, he appeared to be a little shaken in his advocacy of the absolutely 'Free Trade' policy of this country, which Sir Robert Peel inaugurated—in the face of the increasingly-hostile tariffs of other nations—deeming that it was, at all events, debateable as to whether a small tax upon flour would not do more good than harm, and prevent the calamitous disappearance of the hardy agricultural labourers and their families from the country districts of the United Kingdom."

To return to his own words :—

"In the year 1849, it came before my notice that eleven women, principally from the mountains, brought illicit whisky into Bessbrook, concealed in baskets which were apparently filled with calicoes, tapes, and ribbons. By placing a watch over this traffic we succeeded in excluding all these peddlers except one. This widow was a very determined creature, and used to disguise herself in a variety of ways. She became a sort of mythical personage, and for twelve months evaded us; but at last I traced her to her best customer's house, and followed her, sitting down at the fire beside her and chatting, while poking my stick into the basket to find the hidden treasure.   But it was not there. After leaving the house, half an hour did not elapse until it was reported all over the place that she had hoodwinked Mr. Richardson by taking out the gallon of whisky and making a 'stool' of it for herself!   This woman at last emigrated to America, and from that day, as far as we know, there has been no 'sinful stuff' sold at Bessbrook.   Of course I soon became an abstainer myself to encourage our people."

We regret to say that at this point there is an abrupt termination to this little autobiography, but we shall endeavour to continue the history of the founder of Bessbrook, where the great fact has been worked out that a factory population rejoice in the absence of strong drink, and in the happiness and profit its absence confers.   It is also a fact that, while party spirit and sectarian feeling have worked havoc in many parts in Ireland, the people of this Temperance colony, Roman Catholic and Protestant, have lived in harmony, without the crime and disturbance which have desolated other parts of the land. In a letter written to W. E. Gladstone, when in office, we shall once more let the subject of this memorial speak :—

" I am firmly convinced that if the Ministry had done their first work, and had braved the opposition of the spirit trade, they would have had a greater blessing on their labours for Ireland as well as England. It is a well-known fact that not a meeting for rapine and murder takes place in Ireland at which whisky does not play a prominent part, and that our poor countrymen would be incapable of committing the outrages which have taken place without the stimulus of whisky. It is well known, too, that the amount drunk in whisky and beer at least equalled the rental paid during the last three years, and we have proof that where least rent was paid most whisky was sold. God only knows how many murders were hatched in public-houses, or how many publicans licensed by the Government have taken part in the disturbances! *Apropos* of licensed spirit dealers, how is it that no effort has been made even to prevent the increase of a class which, in case of Temperance legislation, you and others have stated would be fairly entitled to compensation ? The effect of this constant increase must surely be a corresponding increase in the liabilities of the nation, not to speak of all the acknowledged evils of which the trade is a fruitful source."

To return to the point where the auto-biography ends, we find J. G. Richardson, in 1847, happily married, occupying himself assiduously in public and commercial affairs, and gaining for himself the reputation of being one of the foremost merchants of the day. Everything had prospered in his hand ; and, guided by a rapidity in forming con-clusions which was certainly more a gift of intuition than due to any lengthened process of reasoning, he had created and built up business concerns and chosen able men to manage them. He had assisted to found the flourishing Inman line of steamers, an enterprise from which, however, he retired in 1854 from conscientious motives, when the owners decided to charter the vessels to carry war stores to the Crimea. Other extensive agencies in Alexandria and Philadelphia were in contemplation, when in this heyday of prosperity and in the strength of manhood he was to hear a Voice speaking above the voices of the world.

That Holy Spirit which had called him to whole-hearted consecration in early life had been in measure silenced, or only attended to at intervals in his busy life. Now, in infinite love, a pause was ordained, and he was arrested in his career. His beloved wife, after only four years of married life, was suddenly snatched from him in 1849, leaving a son and infant daughter; a business panic threatened calamity to his commercial interests, and illness laid its hand upon himself, and he was brought to say : " When Thou with rebukes dost correct man for iniquity, Thou makest his beauty to consume away like a moth ; surely every man is vanity."

In this time of sore affliction he broke up his home in Belfast, and retired with his little boy to live at Lisnagarvey, the home of his eldest sister, Sarah Malcomson, who had in youthful days ministered to the flame of divine love in his soul. In his stricken condition he found in her society, and that of Eli and Sybil Jones (who remained some months with them on account of illness), that quiet and solace needed; here he remembered and renewed vows made in the dew of his youth, that if his Heavenly Father would be with him to forgive and bless, he would henceforth give Him the dominion in his heart, life, and business.

During these years of bereavement and ill-health he withdrew, when still under forty, from the position of leader in business to that of adviser, believing that the Lord required him to be more and more weaned from the spirit of the world, and to serve Him on a higher platform of religion and philanthropy. He had thoughts of retiring altogether from business life, but, in accordance with the counsel of his honoured friend John Hodgkin, he felt that he could best serve his Heavenly Father by still holding his position, while he made it subservient to higher interests. At one period, when ill and almost in despair as to his spiritual state, a beloved uncle, John

Richardson, sent him a text which he felt as a direct message from Heaven : " In a small moment I have forsaken thee, but with great mercy will I gather thee ; in a little wrath I hid My face from thee for a moment, but with everlasting kindness will I have mercy on thee, saith the Lord thy Redeemer."

In 1853 he married Jane M. Wakefield, of Moyallon, County Down, having had, as he believed, the most distinct guidance by the Holy Spirit in taking this important step in life. He settled at Brookhill, near Lisburn, where he devoted himself to country pursuits, affairs of the Society, and benevolent objects, still retaining his business position. Here, as wherever he made his home, he welcomed visitors of all classes, especially keeping open house for the messengers of the Gospel. Jonathan Grubb's visits were a characteristic feature of those days, and were a means of leading him out into a larger place in Christian experience. Being now free from the detail and routine of business, his mind had leisure and opportunity to enter with a wide and increasing interest into all that affected the good of the country and the world at large. Humble and simple as a child in his spiritual life, he held very strong opinions on matters which concerned the social and political well-being of humanity.

His native country engrossed much of his attention, and his life-long desire was to lessen, or, if possible, destroy the power of the factors to which most of her miseries were due. These were strong drink, and the spirit of religious animosity which has in Ireland divided man from man. He felt that if the baneful influence of these two foes to peace and goodness were removed, the third great source of disturbance, political agitation, fomented largely by men who make politics a means of personal gain, would be lessened or destroyed.

Caring as he did for the welfare of his fellows belonging to every class and creed, the extremes of party feeling were particularly distasteful to him. His children were taught to look on exhibitions of party bigotry on either side with impartial disapproval.

To heal the wounds of Ireland and repair her waste places was his dearest wish.

He entered heartily, with John Bright and other lovers of Ireland, into the scheme of Unsectarian National Education which has worked so well for many years, as he felt fully convinced that Protestant and Catholic children, mingling together in school and playground from their earliest years, would not continue to cherish the same bitter animosities which divided their fathers. It was with very great satisfaction that he saw among the names of the original Commissioners of National Education, mingled in harmony of aim, those of Dr. Whately, Protestant Archbishop of Dublin and Primate of Ireland, and of Dr. Murray, Roman Catholic Archbishop and Primate.

In these schools thus inaugurated, which have been such a blessing to the country for many years, half an hour was daily devoted to religious instruction, Protestant and Roman Catholic teachers presiding over their own pupils in separate rooms. In the case of the school having but Protestant teachers, no Roman Catholic children were obliged to attend.

John G. Richardson, and others working on these lines of broad and philanthropic Liberalism, had the comfort of observing, during the 40 years preceding 1886, an unmistakable increase of friendly feeling and reciprocity between Protestants and Roman Catholics.

With W. E. Gladstone's policy, up to its sudden reversal in 1886, he fully sympathized, although deeply regretting his neglect of Temperance legislation, and especially deploring his action with regard to the granting of " Grocers' Licences." The Land Acts for the benefit of the Irish tenant had his active support, though he himself, as a landlord, suffered thereby. By means of these Acts the Irish tenant is in now a more favourable position than any agriculturalist in the civilized world. He rejoiced also in the fact that all political disabilities had been removed from the way of the Roman Catholics.

Anyone who has not watched the gradual fulfilment of the hopes of such Irish philanthropists can scarcely imagine the disappointment and dismay which was felt by his Irish followers when W. E. Gladstone gave in his adhesion to men whose steps he and his fellow-ministers had declared to be " dogged with crime."

John G. Richardson lived to see his views sadly confirmed, for instead of uniting Irishmen, even the foretaste of such a policy has had the effect of undoing the beneficient labours of years. The dying animosity has revived on both sides, and is observable by many indications. The Roman Catholic priests withdrew the Catholic children from the liberalizing influences of common education and created schools of their own.

The Bill of 1893 he did not live to see, but in the face of all the conflict in store for Ireland, we may be thankful that, having " served his own generation by the will of God," he was spared the pain of seeing his fears more fully realized.

About five years after his second marriage the family removed to Moyallon, which brought him within driving distance of Bessbrook. In this colony he continued to take increasing interest as it grew in size and importance

R

until some 3,000 workers were employed. In order to be more among his people, he enlarged a house and made it a residence for part of the year, remodelling and beautifying the grounds, as he had already done in three other places—for he was naturally a gifted landscape-gardener and a lover of flowers.

For many years an Elder in the Society of Friends, his voice was often heard in its meetings, and its welfare had a warm place in his heart. At Bessbrook he built a large Meeting-house, and in a few years gathered quite a colony of Friends. But, although he was strongly attached to the distinguishing views of Friends, his religious sympathy was bounded by no sect or limit, but reached out to and embraced all who loved and served the same blessed Master. A First-day Evening Meeting was begun soon after he settled at Moyallon, held at first in the conservatory, then in a hall built for the purpose. To this, as well as to a large First-day school, all sects and conditions of persons came, and helped in carrying on the work. Many can testify that the whole neighbourhood for miles round felt the influence; and the disappearance of five public-houses was largely due to his efforts. In the words of one who knew him well, we may say: " Praise God for the courage and godly independence with which he stood out for real, soul-converting religion, and resolutely and un-changingly rowed against the opposing current of dead formalism, and the trying influence or quiet opposition of good but mistaken people."

Vocal prayer at family worship was long laid on his heart, but during the earlier period of his family life he had resisted the prompt-ings of the Spirit, and used afterwards to tell how he often went to his room trembling under a sense of unfaithfulness. But in later years his voice was constantly heard at such times in prayer for those he loved, for the work laid upon his heart at Bessbrook and Moyallon, and for the nation at large.

Among other means of caring for the welfare of the people around him, he frequently dis-tributed tracts and periodicals. The " tract-bag " was a well-known institution in his drives between Moyallon and Bessbrook and elsewhere; the appearance of the carriage was

R 2

a signal for the children to run out expecting the usual supply of literature. His ways with children were very sweet, and the little ones in the cottages loved him. His last act on leaving Moyallon, ten days before his death, was to order the horses to stop, that he might hand a gift to the gardener for his little girl, which he had not had time to deliver himself.

We might mention here the pleasure he took in helping young men to start in life, and in assisting others who were in difficulties. Appeals for help were seldom refused, and though sometimes deceived, he was never discouraged:

> " Still a large faith in humankind he cherished,
> And in God's love to all."

From any tale of woe, or the voice of a beggar, he could not bear to turn away, and his lack of self-consciousness in all he did gave an added charm and originality to his acts on behalf of others. With his own hand he would take garments or food to beggars in the conservatory ; and, on one occasion, after giving one man his fare to help him back to London, clothing two or three families, aiding an old man whose daughter had run away, and various other applicants, he came in and said in real perplexity to one of his family: " I wish I could tell why these unfortunate creatures come to *me !* "

It was a happy day for many a family when assisted to go to Bessbrook. In many cases taken out of abject poverty, and given a chance of helping themselves, they have become respectable and respected members of the colony there. His kind and pleasant manner attracted and attached his people and servants to him. After his death, they would say: " It is a father we have lost !"

His deep interest in the social welfare of the people, local and general, continued throughout life. In 1882 he declined a baronetcy, saying, in his letter to W. E. Gladstone, that the " acceptance of the offer, on the ground of his having tried to do a little for the benefit of his fellow-men, would detract from the satisfaction he had found in so doing." In the same letter he again strongly urges that statesman to adopt some decided measure in favour of the Temperance cause.

The cause of peace was very near his heart,

and during his last years he took a great pleasure in extending William Jones's tour to Australia and elsewhere, to advocate the cause of international arbitration.

His last address in Moyallon Meeting was of the nature of a farewell, though he was then in his usual health. He pressed on the young men the sad consequences of permitting the world to occupy the uppermost place in their hearts, and brought his own experience to bear on what he said.

On the 20th of Third Month he was suddenly seized with influenza, which ended, as we reverently believe, in life more abundant, on the 28th. During the sad week of illness at Bessbrook there was a solemn stillness over the place, the people passing one another without the usual greetings, in silent sorrow, for each felt that it was *their* friend who was passing away. Congestion of the lungs had fastened for the third time on his now delicate frame, and during most of the time there was unconsciousness and little or no suffering. His childhood's instinct was strong even in death. On the last evening in which he was able to think consecutively, he desired that something should be given to his night-nurse to read, bearing on the way of salvation through Christ, as he had found that she was a Unitarian. She, like all others in contact with him, became much attached to him on account of his kindness and thought for her comfort. At one time he said he had been thinking of the honour God had put upon us poor creatures in making us "heirs with Himself, and joint heirs with Christ." Frequently he asked for hymns, and was soothed by his favourites, "Rock of Ages," "Jesus, lover of my Soul," and many others. The last one he asked for was the simple hymn beginning: "I am so glad that our Father in Heaven." When the verse was repeated, "My God, I am Thine, what a comfort divine!" he responded with almost his last effort: "Ah, what a comfort!"

As his family were gathered in prayer for a painless departing of the spirit, and in thanksgiving for the victory over death and the grave, the summons came and he fell asleep. "The Lord gave and the Lord hath taken away, blessed be the Name of the Lord."

As the funeral, a mile and a half in length, passed through the country roads to Moyallon, many expressions of deep sorrow were heard. One of his own tenants was overheard to say: " You may talk of the Duke of ——'s death " (a neighbouring landlord), "but what is it to this ? You may expect the great men of your party in Parliament to do wonders for you, but if there were more like Mr. Richardson, who lived among his people, Ireland would soon be a different country."

These particulars are given with no view of bringing honour to him who would have been the first to shrink from the attempt. The honour all belongs to the Master, through Whose grace the servant was enabled in good measure to accomplish the ambition of his childhood and " care for the welfare of the people around him." This little memoir may also shew how human hearts responded to the touch of kindness, and the blessing that followed a life in which such acts were performed spontaneously, naturally, and not on the lines of duty or self-sacrifice.

After his death some memoranda were

found in his desk, referring chiefly to his desire to have a very simple funeral, and written about a year previously. We give extracts :—

" I have lately been brought to think much about funeral arrangements ; indeed, for the greater part of my life I have tried to battle with the way in which working people and those without a shilling to spare involve themselves in funeral expenses. This habit is kept up by the expensive arrangements of the rich, and the time has come when a decided protest should be made by each of us. I therefore wish to set a quiet example with regard to my funeral. I wish no flowers, no outward show of any kind, but a private committal to the grave by and amongst mine own people. I have also felt concerned of late at the difficulty of controlling the ministry at our ' Friends' ' funerals. I feel sure that the ministry would be most telling if the communications were short. Would that my death might be the means of bringing my dear relations and friends to remember that the end of life must come, and that my funeral might be a day of fresh consecration of souls to the service of God, so that in some little measure, my death, like Samson's of olden time, might do more good than my life. My earnest prayer is that all may experience that change of heart which is proved by our love for Him and His cause, who is the Way, the Truth, and the Life. I feel every year more and more that I am nothing, Christ is all; that I am but a monument of Divine Grace; and that I might have lived a far more devoted life to God, my Master, who, I trust, has forgiven and will forgive me, a poor worm of the dust. I rely only upon the mercy of God, through faith in His Blessed Son, the faith in Jesus which gives the victory."

As an instance of the practical way in which from time to time he conveyed instruction, a Friend remembers his addressing our Evening Mission Meeting in somewhat of the following manner:—

"The case of an awakened sinner made sensible by the Holy Spirit of the value of his immortal soul, may not inaptly be compared to a man made aware of the fact that a sum of money had become his. He is now anxious to hand it over to safe keeping. He comes to me for advice with regard to a certain bank. I recommend it, as being highly trustworthy. He appears satisfied and intends to lodge the money there. I meet him in a month and ask if he has carried out his intention. No, the money is still in his pocket. His resolution has never been carried into effect. Through procrastination he runs a great risk, and after a time I find he has lost the money.

" Such will be the fate of the Soul, unless, by a definite act of faith in the trustworthiness of God's promises, we commit the keeping of our immortal part unto Him as unto a faithful Creator and Redeemer."

In the spirit of the above we conclude with Paul's testimony, which may be ours also by faith :

" I know whom I have believed, and am persuaded that He is able to keep that which I have committed unto Him against that day." —2 Tim. i, 12.

We have now brought our task to a

conclusion, having taken up the thread of biography nigh two-and-a-half centuries back, and lived in companionship with many who, with more or less success, helped to make their own day fruitful, and the present what it is for us.

Two convictions are borne in on the mind in making this review: First,—How full of usefulness is life when God's purposes are fulfilled. Through the doing of God's Will man becomes a centre of light and helpfulness, and thus serves his generation in the sphere appointed for the few years of his life below. Second,—We cannot but marvel at the un-merited goodness of the Heavenly Father, and admire the fulfilment of His covenant of mercy in Jesus Christ, as the blessing descends from generation to generation to them who fear Him, and His righteousness to children's children.—Ps. ciii, 17.

When first the thought of gathering together these fragments was presented to the mind, the command—" Ye shall let your children know "—caused it to take shape in the present pages. They were intended as a reminder to the family concerned of their responsibility and privilege, but if these memorials can have any wider range of service they may go forth as a witness to the goodness and mercy of God.

" Know, therefore, that the Lord thy God, He is God, the faithful God, which keepeth covenant and mercy with them that love Him, and keep His commandments, to a thousand generations."— Deut. vii, 9.

THE END.

APPENDICES.

INDEX TO APPENDICES.

APPENDIX A.—George Fox and his Friends.

Under the circumstances narrated in Chapter II, many were prepared for a cordial reception of the mission of George Fox, the founder of the Society of Friends.

Dissatisfied with all that school men and professors of ·religion could do, or say, to meet his anxious and earnest search after truth, when almost in despair, an inward voice bade him turn from man, saying : " There is one, Jesus Christ, who can speak to thy condition." After finding peace through faith in Christ,. " I was sent forth," he writes, " to turn people from darkness to light, that they might receive Christ Jesus to direct them to the Spirit that gave forth the Scriptures, by which they might be led into all truth. I saw that Jesus Christ died for all, and was a propitiation for all. . . I was to bring people off from their own ways to Christ, the new and living way, and from the world teachers, made by man, to learn of Christ, of whom the Father said : ' This is my beloved Son, hear ye Him.' And from the world's worships, that they might worship the Father of Spirits who seeks such to worship Him. I was to call them from the world's religions, that they might know the pure religion, and might visit the fatherless, and the widows, and the strangers, and keep themselves unspotted from the

s

world. I was to bring them off from the world's fellow-ships and prayings and singings, which stood in form, not in power, that their fellowship might be in the Eternal Spirit of God—that they might pray in the Holy Ghost, and sing in the spirit, and with the grace that comes by Jesus, making melody in their hearts unto the Lord. . . . Off from vain traditions and Jewish ceremonies, from men's inventions—worldly doctrines, with ministers of their own making in schools and colleges, who are not of Christ's making—and all vain traditions which the Lord's power was against; in His dread and authority I was moved to declare against them all. . . . And this made the sects and professors rage. But the Lord's power carried me over all, and many were turned to God in a little time, for the heavenly day of the Lord sprung from on high and broke forth apace, and by its light many came to see where they were."

The work thus begun spread with great rapidity. In ten years sixty ministers were sharing in George Fox's commission, and, in the face of bonds and afflic-tions, were bearing testimony to the spirituality of the Gospel Dispensation in almost every country of the known world. Very soon Barbadoes, New England, Virginia, Algiers, Malta, Turkey, Hungary, Germany, France, Austria, Jerusalem, heard the word from these untiring messengers of the Cross.

" Fox himself appealed to all sorts and conditions of men. He admonished Pope Leo XI ; he tried to convert Oliver Cromwell ; he exhorted the Ambassadors of the Great Powers assembled at Nimmeguen to make peace ; he warned the citizens of Oldenburg of their iniquities ; he invoked in thousands of the Yeomanry of England a fervour of spirit almost equal to that which actuated himself, believing they were called to kindle a new life in the dying body of society."* He was enabled to confute many professors of religion in public disputation, and became the means of converting magistrates, priests, and people—some clergymen left valuable livings to follow him.

In about forty years some 100,000 Friends had been gathered into organized and settled churches. During all this time he experienced fierce persecution, which caused much bodily suffering, through long and repeated confinement in different jails of the kingdom. The state of these prisons is not easily conceived ; that of Doomsdale, in Launceston, has never been exceeded for pestilential noisomeness, nor those of Lancaster and Scarborough Castle for exposure to the inclemency of the elements. In the two latter his clothes were scarcely ever dry for two years. This exposure to the severity of the weather laid the foundation, by injuring his health, for future suffering during the remainder of his life. He possessed the most undaunted courage, for he feared no earthly power, and was never deterred from attending meetings, though he knew officers would be

---

* Hepworth Dixon.

S 2

there to seize his person. In his conversations with Oliver Cromwell, or in his letters to the Parliament, or to King Charles II, or to any other personage, he displayed his usual boldness of character, and never lost, by means of any degrading flattery, his dignity as a man.

At one time King Charles was so touched with the hardship of his case that he offered to discharge him from prison by pardon, but George Fox declined, for the reason that, as pardon implied guilt, his innocence would be called in question by his acceptance of it. So he lay in jail until his trial, when, upon errors in his indictment, he was discharged in an honourable way.

After nearly fifty years of missionary travel, labour, and suffering he died in London, in the sixty-seventh year of his age, two days after attending a great meeting in Gracechurch Street. William Penn says: " As he lived, so he died; so full of assurance was he, that he triumphed over death, as if it was scarce worth a notice or a mention: near the last recommending the despatch of an epistle." The last letter written before his busy pen was laid down was to comfort and support Friends in Ireland under their sufferings. " Mind," said he, " poor Friends in Ireland and America." On inquiry being made " how he found himself?" his reply was: " Never heed, the Lord's power is over all weakness and death; the seed reigns. Blessed be the Lord!"

The persecution of the Quakers continued from 1650 to the time of the Act of Toleration granted to Protestant dissenters in the first year of William and Mary, in 1689.

Joseph Besse says, in his " Collection of the Sufferings of the People called Quakers" (two large volumes) : " Under this state of persecution, wherein Friends were exercised from infancy, their numbers greatly increased, so that it might be said of them as of the Israelites in Egypt : ' The more they afflicted them the more they multiplied and grew.' For Religion, next to her own light and energy on the heart of man, has not a stronger argument in her favour than the patience and constancy of her afflicted confessors."

A brotherly love and sympathy was very remarkable in this people, some of whom travelled hundreds of miles to visit and minister to their brethren in prison. While they seemed regardless of their own liberty, they were incessant in representing to those in authority the suffering case of their Friends. A printed paper was presented to the Parliament in 1659, and subscribed to by 164 Friends wherein they make an offer of their own bodies, person for person, to lie in prison instead of such of their brethren as were then under confinement in danger of their lives through extreme durance. It runs thus :

" Friends, who are called a Parliament of this nation : We, in love to our brethren who are in houses of correction—many in fetters and irons, cruelly beaten by savage gaolers, and many persecuted to death, dying in prison, many lying sick and weak on straw—

we, in love to our brethren, do offer up our own bodies and selves to you to put us into the same dungeons, on their straw, and into their nasty holes and prisons; we do stand ready sacrifices to take their places, that they may go forth and not die in prison, for many of the brethren are dead already. . . . And if you will receive our bodies, we freely tender them to you for our Friends who are in bondage for speaking the truth, for not paying tithes, for meeting together in the fear of God, for refusing to swear, for being accounted as vagrants, for wearing the hat, for visiting their friends. We, whose names are hereunto subscribed, are waiting in Westminster Hall for an answer from you to us to answer our tenders."

Here follow the names of 164 brave and devoted Friends, a muster roll precious in the sight of their God, though little esteemed among men.

During the time of George Fox's imprisonment in Launceston Jail, a friend offered himself "To lie in Doomsdale Dungeon in his stead." It was not allowed, but, on this occasion, Cromwell asked some of his council: "Which of you would do as much for me?"

William Dewsbury, second only to George Fox in labours and sufferings, lay 19 years in Warwick Prison, four of them in a dungeon 12 feet under ground, with a cesspool in the middle. "Few ever came out in health," quietly observed the Friends who wrote at this time. W. Dewsbury's little grand-daughter, of 12 years of age, who, under a sense of duty came to wait on him in confinement, took ill, and on her death-bed spoke to those around like an experienced Christian.

Sewell's "History of the Quakers," exhibits such a scene of savage persecution on the one hand, and firmness and patience on the other, as is not easily paralleled.

"At one time, there were few of them except those below the cognizance of the magistrates, who were not in prison for their faith." About the year 1662, persecution ran very high in England and Wales, so that upwards of 4,200 Quakers were in prisons of the vilest description.

But the malice of persecution did not stop here; the property of the most respectable families was confiscated, and a great number died of maltreatment.

The worst outrages were, however, perpetrated in New England, by those who had themselves fled from persecution in their native land—among many other instances, three Quaker women were stripped to the waist and beaten. On Boston Common, in 1660, Mary Dyer sealed her testimony with her blood. It not often falls to the lot of one individual to be twice brought as a martyr to the place of execution, but such was the fact in the case of this brave woman, before she died by the hands of the common hangman. She is described as being "Comely and of a grave countenance, of a good family and estate," comfortably married and the mother of several children.

It appears that her home was in Rhode Island, and

that she had joined the new Society during a temporary sojourn in England. A Friend named Ann Burden, a widow with children depending on her, wishing to go to America to collect some debts, Mary Dyer, ignorant of the severe laws recently passed against the Quakers, accompanied her. On landing at the Port of Boston, they were at once thrown into prison, from which Mary Dyer was liberated by the exertions of her husband, who had to become " Bound in a great penalty not to lodge her in any town of the colony, nor permit any to have speech with her on her journey."

The recollection of what she had previously endured was, doubtless, still vividly before her when two years afterwards she felt that the Lord called her to go again to Boston, where two young Englishmen of the same religious profession, William Robinson and Marmaduke Stevenson, were then in prison for conscience's sake. Mary Dyer, as we might expect, was again imprisoned, and when at length the three friends were set free, they were forbidden under pain of death to return to the city. Vain, however, were the laws of man to deter these soldiers of the Cross from obeying the orders of their Captain ; they returned, ere long, to bear witness for their Lord in Boston.

After her two companions were condemned to be executed, Mary Dyer was brought before the relentless Endicott. On receiving her sentence, she said : " The will of the Lord be done," and as she went forth to prison, to await her execution, she uttered speeches of praise to the Lord, being full of joy.

Mary Dyer was led out with her companions to the place of execution on Boston Common. "With great cheerfulness they went," says Sewel, "as to an everlasting wedding feast," with "glorious signs of heavenly joy and gladness in their countenances." What mattered to them the two hundred armed men and the noise of the drummers who were ordered to drown their voices? The exalting martyr seemed already among the saints in light. "This is to me," she said "an hour of the greatest joy I could have in this world. No eye can see, no ear can hear, no tongue can utter, and no heart can understand the sweet incomes and refreshings of the Spirit of the Lord, which now I eel." After seeing the dead bodies of those with whom she had lately held sweet fellowship, she mounted the fatal ladder. But just before the accomplishment of the final deed, a cry was heard: "Stop, for she is reprieved." Her feet were loosed, and she was told to come down, but the return to earth from the very portals of heaven was not a thing she had desired. She stood still, and calmly said she was there willing to suffer as her brethren did, unless they would annul their wicked law.

It appeared that her son had interceded for her life, but it was a forfeited life still, and she was remanded to prison.

The people at Boston were more compassionate than

their rulers. Many of them were aroused to indignation at the death of two good men like Stevenson and Robinson, and in order to calm them it was thought expedient to send Mary Dyer to her home, so she was put on horseback, and escorted fourteen miles on her return journey towards Rhode Island. The following year, however (1660), she felt called once more to go back, and remonstrate against the unrighteous and unjust laws.

Being summoned before the General Court, she undauntedly owned herself to be the same Mary Dyer who had been sentenced before by the same tribunal. Governor Endicott, doubtless enraged to see that his laws availed nothing with this courageous woman, allowed her only a few hours to await the carrying out of her sentence of death. But this was no trouble to her, of whom one of her fellow-labourers gave a similar testimony to that which we read of the first martyr: " She even shined in the image of God."

From an earthly prison to a heavenly mansion was a royal passage, though the way might be rough. When offered her life if she would return, her reply was ready: " Nay, I cannot, for in His will I abide faithful to death." " I have been in Paradise several days," were some of her last words. A moment under the rough hand of the executioner, and then present with her God.

In the year 1661, after the cruel treatment thus inflicted upon the Quakers at Boston, Elizabeth Hutton, one of George Fox's first converts, believed herself called to proceed there and witness against these wicked laws.

When carried before Governor Endicott, he asked, with much abuse, what she and her companion came there for. Elizabeth answered : " To warn thee, that thou shed no more innocent blood." They were conveyed to prison, but afterwards were taken two day's journey to a desolate wilderness, infested by bears and wolves, and left there to take chance of life or death. Through the protecting hand of their God they got from thence to Rhode Island. But returning to Boston she was ordered to be whipped as a vagrant, which order was executed in several towns, after which, being left again in a wilderness, she made her way to her friends, giving thanks to God, who had counted her worthy to suffer for His name. In after years we find this record by George Fox's pen : " About a week after we landed in Jamaica, Elizabeth Hutton, a woman of great age, who had travelled much in Truth's service, and suffered much for it, departed this life. She was well the day before she died, and went in peace like a lamb, bearing testimony to Truth at her departure."

The early Evangelistic stage of the Society produced many women who received a share in proclaiming the Gospel in its simplicity and spirituality. On the subject of the ministry of woman, Barclay, in his " Apology," Proposition X, says :

" Seeing male and female are one in Christ Jesus, and that He gives His Spirit no less to one than to the other, when God moveth by His Spirit in a woman, we judge it no ways unlawful for her to preach in the assemblies of God's people.

"Neither think we that of Paul, 1 Cor., xiv, 34, to reprove the inconsiderate and talkative women among the Corinthians, who troubled the Church of Christ with their unprofitable questions, or 1 Tim., ii, 11-12, that women ought to learn in silence, not usurping over the man, anyways repugnant to this doctrine.

" Because it is clear that women have prophesied and preached in the Church, else had that saying of Joel been ill applied by Peter, Acts ii, 17.

" And seeing Paul himself in the same Epistle to the Corinthians giveth rules how women should behave themselves in their public preaching and praying, it would be a manifest contradiction if that other place were taken in a larger sense.

" And the same Paul speaks of a woman that laboured with him in the work of the Gospel, and it is written that Philip had four daughters that prophesied.

" And lastly it hath been observed that God hath effectually in this day converted many souls by the ministry of women, and by them also frequently comforted the souls of His children, which manifest experience puts the thing beyond all controversy."

Margaret Fell, the wife of Judge Fell, who was married to George Fox after eleven years of widowhood, was a zealous preacher and able writer. She suffered two imprisonments, and three times did she journey from her northern home to plead with King Charles on behalf of the suffering Quakers. She died in much peace at Swartenmore, aged 86, having survived her husband twelve years.

Among other women who laboured in the Gospel were Catherine Evans and Sarah Chevers, called, as they believed, to Alexandria. They were arrested at Malta, and suffered a fearful imprisonment in the Inquisition, which lasted four years. One man died from torture in the Inquisition in Rome.

It appears that in 1656 Friends first found their way to America. Mary Fisher, accompanied by Anne Austin, who had left behind in London a husband and five children, sailed from Barbadoes to Massachusetts Bay. After suffering severe imprisonments in Boston, they were shipped back to Barbadoes under strict guard. But scarcely had the vessel left the port when another arrived from London, bringing eight more ministers of the Gospel to suffer in their turn.

Mary Fisher, soon after her return to England, entered once more an untrodden path. She sailed for Smyrna, with a message to deliver to Mahomet IV, encamped with his army near Adrianople. On reaching Smyrna she was stopped by the English Consul and sent back to Venice, from whence she made her way by land to Adrianople, preserved from peril and abuse through a journey of 500 miles. On her arrival she requested to be accompanied to the camp. The citizens whom she consulted, fearing the Sultan's displeasure, declined to do so, and Mary Fisher therefore went to the camp alone. When the Grand Vizier heard that there was an English woman who had a message from the Great God to the Sultan, he sent her word that she might speak to him next morning. On returning to the camp at the hour appointed, the Sultan, attended by his great officers of state, sent for her, and asked if it were true that she had a message from the Lord. Mary Fisher answered in the affirmative, upon which he bade her speak on, as she remained silent, with her soul waiting on God, the Sultan supposed she was oppressed with awe, in the presence of such an assembly, and asked her whether she desired that any of the company should retire? She answered: " Nay." He then desired her to speak the Word of the Lord, and not to fear, for they had good hearts, and charged her to speak the Lord's Word, neither more or less, for they were willing to hear it. They all gave attention, with much gravity, till she had concluded, when the Sultan enquired if she had any more to say. She asked if he had understood what she had said? He replied : " Yea, every word," and added, that it was the truth, and desired her to stay in his country, for they could not but respect one who had endured so much and had come so far to carry them the Lord's message. This kindness she modestly declined, as also an escort to Constantinople. He reminded her it was a very dangerous journey, especially for such a maiden, and wondered she had passed so far in safety ; and it was out of respectful concern he offered her a guard, as he would not on any consideration have an injury befall her in his dominions. They then asked what she thought of their prophet, Mahomet, she made a cautious reply that she knew him not, but she knew Christ, the true prophet, the Son of God, who enlighteneth every man that cometh into the world, and added : " If the word of a prophet come to pass then ye shall know the Lord hath sent that prophet, but if it come not to pass then ye shall know the Lord never sent him "; to which they assented, and acknowledged it to be truth. And so she departed without a guard, and reached England safely, having experienced neither injury nor insult. This reception of the infidel Sultan contrasts favourably with that which Christian New England accorded her, and other early Friends.

APPENDIX B.—A SPECIAL PROVIDENCE DURING JAMES DICKINSON'S TRAVELS IN SCOTLAND.

A REMARKABLE circumstance befell James Dickinson and Jane Fearon, while travelling in Gospel service through Scotland, of which we find the following account :—

" Evening approaching, after a tempestuous day, they wished to stop for the night in a small public-house, but their hired guide objected; they could not, however, well understand his dialect, and, being wet and weary, they discharged him and entered the inn. After a short time they became painfully apprehensive that the people of the house had a design upon their lives, and, although they behaved with apparent kindness and attention, these uncomfortable feelings increased. The Friends saw three men about, who were heard to say: ' They have good horses and saddle-bags,' and another added : ' Aye, and good clothes too.'

" The lonely situation of the house and other appearances seemed favourable to the wicked designs of the people. James Dickinson, having seen to the horses, enquired for a room, in which he walked up and down, while his companion broke into tears, saying : ' I fear these men have a design on our lives.' Her companion answered : ' They have mischief in their hearts, but I

hope the Lord will deliver us ; if so, we must run.'
Then James Dickinson, taking the candle carefully and
examining the room, discovered a door, which he opened,
and perceived a stone staircase leading outside the
house.

" Upon this discovery, putting off their shoes they
descended softly, leaving the candle burning in the room.
After running a considerable time they found a building
which they entered ; but soon James Dickinson said :
' We are not safe here, we must run again,' to which his
friend answered : ' I am so weary, I think I cannot go any
further.' She, however, endeavoured to proceed till
they came to a river near the south coast. On passing
along they came to a bridge, but, attempting to go over
James Dickinson said : ' We must not go over this
bridge, but go further up the river side.' This they did,
and sat down.

" After some time he grew uneasy, and said : ' We
must wade through the water.' Jane Fearon replied :
' Alas ! how can we cross the river, knowing not its
depth ? rather wait and let us see what they will be
permitted to do ; it will be better for them to take our
lives than for us to drown ourselves.' But James said :
' Fear not, I will go before thee !' upon which they
entered the river and got safe through. Walking on
they came to a sand bank, and sat down. But not
feeling easy yet, they arose.

" Proceeding further, they found another sand bank
with a cavity. After a while James said : ' Now we are

T

safe, and in my heart is a song of thanksgiving and praise.'

" When they had been there some time they heard a noise of people on the other side of the river, and fearing they should be discovered, James Dickinson said : 'Our lives now depend on our silence.' Attentively hearkening, they could hear the men say : ' Seek them, Keeper ! ' They believed they were the men seen in the inn. The dog would not go over the bridge, but followed the scent up the stream to the place they crossed. The people repeatedly cried : ' Seek them, Keeper ! ' which they not only heard, but saw the men with a lantern. One said : ' They have crossed the river ! ' another replied : ' That is impossible, unless the Devil took them over, for the river is brink full.' After a considerable time they left, and the Friends saw them no more.

" When the day dawned, a man appeared on a hill at some distance, searching apparently for some one, and they apprehended it was for them. Some time after sunrise they discovered that under the first sandbank they could have been seen from the other side of the river, while their last refuge shaded them from observation.

" Upon considering what they should do to recover their horses and saddle-bags, James Dickinson said : ' I incline to return to the inn, fully believing our belongings will be ready for us.' Jane Fearon replied : ' I dare not go back ' ; upon which James said : ' Thou mayst safely, for I have seen that which has never failed me.' Upon which they returned—no one being in the house but an old woman sitting in a nook by the fireside. The horses were in a stable, which they mounted and departed.

" Some time after, James Dickinson going that way, found the house had been searched, and a number of human bones found. Some of the people were executed, and the inn ordered to be pulled down. It lay there a heap of rubbish."—*Friends' Select Miscellanies.*

T 2

APPENDIX C.—WILLIAM GOFFE.

From " National Dictionary of Biography."

" In 1642 Goffe was imprisoned by the Royalist Lord Mayor for promoting a petition in support of the Parliament's claims to the militia. In 1645, his name appears in the list of the New Model, as captain in Harley's Regiment, and as one of the deputation which presented the charge of the eleven members, July, 1647.

" Goffe was a prominent figure in the Prayer Meeting, when it was decided to bring the King to a trial. He was named one of the Judges, sat frequently during the trial, and signed the King's death warrant.

" In December, 1653, he aided Colonel White to expel the remnant of the Barebones Parliament. In December, 1655, he was appointed Major-General for Berkshire, etc. A large amount of his correspondence is printed in the Thurlow papers, and proves that while active on behalf of the Government he was less arbitrary than many of his colleagues.

" The ' Second Narrative of the Late Parliament' describes Goffe as in ' so great esteem and favour at Court that he is judged the only fit man to have Major Lambert's place and command, as major-general of the army, and, having so far advanced, is in a fair way to the Protectorship hereafter.' He was one of nine persons on the important committee appointed in June, 1658, to consider what should be done in the next Parliament.

"Goffe was one of the persons summoned by Cromwell during his last illness to receive his declarations respecting his successor. He subscribed to the proclamation declaring Richard Cromwell Protector.

"On November 15th, 1658, Richard granted Goffe Irish lands to the value of £500 per annum in fulfilment of his father's intentions.

"Before the Restoration actually took place, April 16th, 1660, a warrant was issued for Goffe's arrest, probably on suspicion that he was concerned in Lambert's intended rising. He succeeded, however, in escaping, but a proclamation offered £100 for his arrest.

"In company with his father-in-law, Lieutenant-General Whalley, Goffe landed at Boston, Massachusetts, in July, 1660. under the name of Stephenson, making no other attempt to conceal his identity.

"It was deposed by a certain John Crowne that the Governor, John Endicott, embraced them, and bade them welcome to New England, and wished more such good men would come over.

"They staid for a time at Cambridge, ' where they were held in exceeding high esteem for their piety and parts,' but being, after a time, hotly pursued by order of the English Government, they moved from place to place, and at last to the Rev. John Russell's house at Hadley, in October, 1664.

" Goffe seems to have died in 1679 ; his last letter was dated April 2nd in that year. His correspondence with his wife was conducted as a son to a mother, under the pseudonyms of Frances and Walter Goldsmith, it shews him to have been a man of deep and enthusiastic religious feeling, and explains much relating to his political actions.

" Three of the city avenues at Newhaven, Connecticut, are called respectively, Goffe, Whalley, and Dixwell."

The following is extracted from Anthony Wood's " Athenæ Oxoniensis " and " Fasti Oxoniensis":—

" William Goffe, son of Stephen Goffe, and younger brother of John, was apprenticed to one Vaughan, a salter, in London, brother of Colonel Jos. Vaughan, a Parliamentarian and zealous Presbyterian. Goffe became a common soldier, and was finally promoted to the rank of Colonel. In 1649 he was one of the Judges of King Charles I, and agreed, by standing up and bowing his head, to the sentence of death. In 1654 he, with Colonel White, brought musqueteers and turned out the Anabaptist members which were left behind in the Little, or Barebones, Parliament. Made by Cromwell Major-General of Hampshire, Sussex, and Berks—a place of great profit. Afterwards became Major-General of the Army of Foot, and it was said the Protectorate was settled on him for some future time. He was raised to the Upper House. In 1660 he betook himself to his heels to save his neck, and afterwards, with other Regicides, lived several years in vagabondage."

The following is a copy of the Proclamation Form of arrest from the Guildhall Library :—

"By the King.

"A Proclamation

"for Apprehension of Edward Whalley and William Goffe

"CHARLES R.

"Forasmuch as Edward Whalley, commonly known by the name of Colonel Whalley, and William Goffe, commonly called Colonel Goffe, are, amongst others, by an Act of this present Parliament, entitled 'An Act of free and general pardon, indemnity and oblivion,' wholly excepted from pardon and left to be proceeded against as traytors for their execrable treasons in sentencing to death, signing the instrument for the horrid murder, or being instrumental in taking away the precious life of Our late Dear Father, of blessed memory.

"And forasmuch as they, the said Edward Whalley and William Goffe, having absented themselves, withdrawn themselves and fled, as we have been informed, to the parts beyond the seas, and are now, as we certainly understand, lately returned into Our Kingdom of England, and do privately lurk and obscure themselves in places unknown : We therefore have thought fit, by and with the advice of Our Privy Council, to publish the same to all our loving subjects, not doubting their care and forwardness in their apprehension ; and we do hereby require and command as well, all and singular, our judges, justices of the peace, mayors, sheriffs, bailiffs, constables, and head boroughs, as also the officers and ministers of our ports and other our subjects whatsoever within Our realms of England, Scotland and Ireland, and Our dominion of Wales, and all other Our dominions and territories, to be diligent in inquiring, searching, or seizing and apprehending them, the said Edward Whalley and William Goffe, in all places whatsoever, as well within liberties as without, whom, if they shall happen to take and apprehend, our further will and pleasure is that they cause them, or either of them so apprehended, to be safely carried to the next justice of the peace to where they or either of them shall be arrested, and whom we straitly command to commit them or either of them to prison, and presently inform us and our Privy Council of their or either of their apprehension.

" And we do hereby further declare and publish that if any person or persons after this our Proclamation published, shall directly or indirectly conceal, harbour, keep, retain or maintain the same Edward Whalley or William Goffe, or either of them, or shall contrive or connive at any means whereby they or either of them shall or may escape from being taken or arrested, or shall not use their best endeavour for their or either of their apprehensions, as well by giving due advertisement thereof to Our officers as by all other good means, we will, as there is just cause, proceed against them that shall so neglect this Our commandment with all due severity.

" And lastly, we do hereby declare that whosoever shall discover the said Edward Whalley or William Goffe, either within our Kingdom of England, Scotland, Ireland, or Dominion of Wales, or in any other Our dominions or territories, or elsewhere, and shall cause them or either of them to be apprehended and brought in alive, or dead if they or either of them attempting resistance happen to be slain, shall have a reward of one hundred pounds in money for each of them so brought in dead or alive as aforesaid, to be forthwith paid unto him in recompence of such his service.

"Given at our Court at Whitehall the Two and Twentieth day of September, in the Twelfth Year of Our Reign.

" London : Printed by Christopher Barker and John Bill, Printers to the King's Most Excellent Majesty, 1660."

APPENDIX D.—JAMES NAYLOR'S DYING TESTIMONY.

" THERE is a spirit which I feel that delights to do no evil, nor to revenge any wrong, but delights to endure all things, in hope to enjoy its own at the end. Its hope is to outlive all wrath and contention, and to weary out all exaltation and cruelty, or whatsoever is of a nature contrary to itself. It sees to the end of all temptation; as it bears no evil in itself, so it conceives none in thought to any other. If it be betrayed, it bears it; for its ground and spring is the mercies and forgiveness of God. Its crown is meekness, its life is everlasting love unfeigned, and takes its kingdom with entreaty and not with contention, and keeps it by lowliness of mind.

" In God alone it can rejoice, though none else regard it, or can own its life. It is conceived in sorrow and brought forth without any to pity it, nor doth it murmur at grief and oppression. It never rejoiceth but through suffering, for with the world's joy it is murdered. I found it alone, being forsaken; I have fellowship therein with them who live in dens and desolate places in the earth, who through death obtained this resurrection and eternal holy life."

APPENDIX E.—THE HUGUENOTS AND THE LINEN TRADE IN IRELAND.

THE direful storm of persecution which swept over France and the Netherlands compelled a hardy, God-fearing and industrious people to find refuge in England and Ireland, where they might worship God according to the reformed religion they carried with them—a faith and practice that became a great blessing to the land of their adoption. Perhaps the brightest record we have at this period in the annals of Ireland was the settling down of these outcast Huguenots, to introduce new trades, and, in the midst of strife and party spirit, to live quiet, consistent Christian lives.

The Duke of Alva, in the Low Countries, and the Queen Mother, in France, vied with each other in doing their utmost with the pitiless weapons that fanaticism puts into the hands of Rome.

The Council of Trent, in 1545, sat eighteen years to codify the laws of the Romish Church. The results were statutes clearly setting forth the religious and ecclesiastical faith of Christendom. From these many texts could be gathered which justified any method of diffusing the true belief and exterminating the false. It was decided religion must be honoured by the intro-duction of the Inquisition and a general massacre of heretics in every land.

A few months later, Philip of Spain, under the ferocious Alva, began his bloodthirsty career in the Netherlands; in regard to which, he boasted he had sent 18,000 to the scaffold, besides the immense number killed in battle.

Catherine de Medici pondered this object lesson, and when seven years had passed and the Huguenots were still unsubdued, occasion was found, in 1572, of attracting all the chief Huguenots to Paris, by her invitation to attend the marriage of the Huguenot Prince, Henry of Navarre, with her daughter Margaret.

In the midst of feast and friendship, the tocsin sounded, and the murderers were let loose all over Paris.   Hospitality, relationship, youth, sex, were all disregarded; the streets ran with blood, and the river was choked with mutilated bodies.   No pen can picture the horrors of St. Bartholomew's Day.   Sully says 70,000 Protestants perished during that August, 1572, and a Roman Catholic Bishop stated the number to be 100,000.

Pope Gregory XIII, who was privy to the plot, celebrated a *Te Deum* on hearing the news, and proclaimed a Jubilee over the whole Christian world, and a solemn procession, in which he took part, to thank God for this glorious success.   A messenger was despatched to Paris to congratulate the King, and give the assassins his blessing.*

Huguenot emigrants of all classes fled in open boats

---

* See *Eighteen Christian Centuries* —White

across the channel, and found a retreat on the shore of England; a large proportion were industrious trades-men, who had read the newly-translated Bible in their own tongue, and renounced the errors of the papal system.

Sir Thomas Gresham, writing from Antwerp, in 1566, said : " There are here above 40,000 who will rather die than have the Word of God put to silence."

Leaving the busy quays deserted, and most of their property in the hand of the spoiler, merchants and men came to lay the foundation of industries in other lands.

The Massacre in France was the cause, as we have seen, of another invasion, but our brief notice rests with the Refugees who reached Ireland, and established the linen trade in that distracted country.

So early as 1590, Sir Henry Sidney mentions a small colony settled in County Dublin, diligently employed in making diaper, ticks, and other stuffs for men's use, and tanning leather of deer skins.

In the reign of Charles I, Chief Deputy the Earl of Stafford applied himself with much zeal, and used his own private means to establish the linen industry, though it was afterwards made one of the grounds of his im-peachment that he had obstructed trade by introducing new and unknown processes in the manufacture of flax.

The Duke of Ormond followed his example by induc-ing Refugees to settle in Ireland. Many were pursuing peaceably their respective trades, when, in the revolution of 1688, Ireland became the scene once more of confusion and civil war, which continued to the detriment of trade and progress until the Peace of Limerick, 1691, when William III took measures to restore the prostrate industry of the country.

Naturalization was granted to those refugees who would settle in Ireland, with freedom to exercise their religion, of which many took advantage.

The northern counties of Down and Antrim were, however, more than any other, regarded as the sanctuary of the Refugees. There they settled among men of their own faith, who had fled from the Stuart persecution in Scotland to take refuge in the comparatively unmolested districts of Ulster.

Lisburn, seven miles south of Belfast, was one of their favourite settlements; the place, with many others, had been burnt to the ground in the civil war of 1641.

But under the encouragement of the Government, and in the hands of a busy and God-fearing people, it, ere long, became a flourishing place of trade and linen industry.

Thus in great measure began the prosperity of Protestant Ulster, the chief seat of commerce in due time being moved to Belfast.

And here we may learn afresh the lesson, that there is no evil so terrible out of which God cannot work good. For we see in the history of the Scotch, French, and Low Country Refugees evidence that a blessing to themselves and to their adopted country followed their faithfulness to God.

See pages **APPENDIX F.**   193-6.

In order that the ground of this separation may not be misunderstood, we give the following extract from the Minute of London Yearly Meeting of 1829, in relation to this subject.

After concluding not to hold any correspondence with the section of " Friends " in Baltimore Yearly Meeting referred to, the Minute continues :—

" This step is taken under a feeling of painful concern for those who have recognized a body of separatists in Pennsylvania ' who have denied the proper divinity of our Lord and Saviour Jesus Christ, and whose aim has been much directed against the virtue and benefit of that most satisfactory sacrifice, which He made of Himself when He was crucified without the gates of Jerusalem ' (see the Epistle from the Meeting for Sufferings in Philadelphia, Eleventh Month 23, 1827).   And this Meeting feels a warm desire that it may please the Lord in His abundant mercy to enable them clearly to see that blessing which He has provided for the whole human race in His beloved Son, our Lord and Saviour Jesus Christ, Who died for our sins and rose again for our justification ; ' in Whom dwelleth all the fulness of the God-head bodily,' and Whose glorious divinity is set forth in this declaration of the Evangelist : ' In the beginning was the Word, and the Word was with God, and the Word was God ; all things were made by Him, and without Him was not anything made that was made ' ; ' And the Word was made flesh, and dwelt amongst us, and we beheld His glory, the glory as of the only begotten of the Father, full of grace and truth.' "   See also Declaratory Minute of same year in London Book of Discipline.